Where the River Takes Me

The Hudson's Bay Company
Diary of Jenna Sinclair

BY JULIE LAWSON

Scholastic Canada Ltd.

*Fort Edmonton,
Saskatchewan District*

Friday, August 31st, 1849

I begin with an Adventure!

This morning Suzanne and I walked out to the lake where her cousins were fishing, and made off with their ponies!

Oh, *mon dieu,* already I am guilty of Exaggeration, for we did not *take* the ponies, but did sneak up on them with great stealth and daring to see if we could touch them without the boys noticing — and we succeeded! If we were not forbidden to ride the ponies, we could have ridden them anywhere! (And if we knew how.)

The boys were so engaged in their fishing we then succeeded in sneaking up on them — but ran off before their embarrassment at having been caught unawares turned to anger.

Off we ran to untie our imaginary ponies. Then we galloped like mischief across the wide-open prairie, our hair flying in the wind and our voices bursting forth with wild whoops of victory!

And now I am thinking, if only we had broken the rule and taken the boys' ponies, even to sit on one for a *moment,* for I may never have another chance — because Aunt Grace is getting married and we are moving to another Fort!

Mon dieu, what an extraordinary day. An Adventure (of sorts) followed by two surprising announcements.

I have been waiting for such a day, when something happens beyond the usual chores, activities and pastimes, the comings and goings of buffalo, Indians, brigades, missionaries and visitors — and now that the day has finally arrived, I have started my brand new Journal. Except mine will be different from the Official Post Journal that is sent to London each year, because instead of writing the Daily Accounts of weather, crops, livestock, provisions, etc., I'm going to write about Adventures.

It's hard to believe that it is almost a year since I found this Journal, when I was sorting through Father's things. At the time I was too shaken by his death to even think of writing, and I should have given it to Aunt Grace, what with paper being so scarce, but the Journal seemed to cry out, "I've been put aside for you, Jenna." Father knew I loved to write, and I think he would have been pleased that the opening pages mark not a sad ending but a new beginning.

Aunt Grace would not approve of my keeping it without asking her permission. In her view it would be akin to *stealing* — a Misdemeanor of the Gravest Sort — but as she is presently out walking with her husband-to-be, it is safe for me to write without fear of being discovered. I do not want her to mark *another* Misdemeanor against my name — though perhaps she will clear the slate in celebration of her marriage.

I am wandering off the track (another Misdemeanor), so back to the day's events.

Suzanne and I returned to the Fort in time for Dinner, and spent most of the afternoon in the Home Guard camp helping Nokum and the other women make pemmican. I love being there, close to Nokum, listening to all the gossip and stories. Sometimes the women lower their voices to keep the girls from hearing, but it only makes us listen harder!

Aunt Grace is fortunate that she's able to teach to earn her keep, for she would *hate* making pemmican. She claims that the slightest whiff of melted fat and dried buffalo meat makes her nauseous. It makes me hungry!

When I returned to our quarters to wash for Supper, Aunt took me by the shoulders, her eyes sparkling — yes, sparkling — and said, "Jenna, I am going to marry Mr. Kennedy!"

"Mr. Kennedy the blacksmith?" I was astounded. My uppity aunt, marrying a *tradesman*? Why would she settle for less than a high-ranking officer?

"The very one!" she says.

"When?"

"In five days!" she says.

"Five days?"

"Aye, Jenna!" By then her brogue was getting stronger, a sure sign she was in a state of high excitement. I teased her about it, the way Father used to do, and she laughed and said that if "dear Robbie" had heard the news, *his* brogue would have been impossible to understand.

True enough! I can imagine him saying, "Nae, Lassie, it canna be! Your aunt's finally found a husband to her liking?"

I remember the times he'd introduce her to a suitable bachelor, but there was always some fault. Too vulgar! Too homely! Too fond of drink! And Father would laugh and say, "She'll only have an Orkneyman like her brother — handsome, hard-working, thrifty and usually sober."

Now she has her Orkneyman, and does not seem to mind that he is stout and bowlegged. Poor Mr. Kennedy. Does he know about her List of Misdemeanors? Perhaps she will make one for husbands!

Aunt Grace's second big announcement is that we are moving.

"Moving?"

"Aye, lass," she says, and tells me to close my gap before the flies move in.

Well, it turns out that Mr. Kennedy has been posted to Fort Colvile. Aunt says it's a good ways away, and our journey will require many weeks of travel. I am certain that each day will bring an Adventure, fit to be recorded in my Journal.

And now I must close, for night has fallen and there is movement afoot in the corridor.

Saturday, September 1st

This morning — even before the clanging of the wake-up bell — I went with Nokum to pick the last of the saskatoon berries.

As we were starting out she said, "This is the last time I walk out on the prairie."

"You say that every time," I teased. But almost at once my laughter gave way to sadness, for I was thinking, How can I leave my grandmother?

We found a few patches of late berries and began to fill our bags. Nokum was quiet, but I chattered away about everything — ponies, buffalo, berries, Aunt's wedding — anything to avoid telling her about the move to Fort Colvile, for fear I would cry.

My bag was almost full when Nokum told me how much I reminded her of my mother. She too was a "little squirrel," never restful, always in a hurry, always talking — the only time she was silent was when she was eating or thinking or sleeping — and sometimes, not even then. It made me think that Nokum was not talking about my mother, but telling me, in a roundabout way, to give her some peace.

On the way back, she drew a pair of moccasins from her pouch and handed them to me, saying that my mother had made them when she was my age.

She had embroidered them too, not with glass beads from the Trade Store but with porcupine quills she had dyed herself. "She had to concentrate," Nokum said, and added with a chuckle, "It was a quiet time."

I hugged the moccasins and could no longer hold back the tears. Nokum told me that she knew I was going away — I should have suspected as much, from her quiet manner — and, as she was wiping the tears from my cheeks, she made me promise not to worry. (A promise I will not be able to keep.) She assured me she was content in the Home Guard camp, living with her sister and her family and having so many other relatives and friends close by. And though her "twitchy joints and achy old bones" had long ago told her she could no longer follow the buffalo with the rest of her family, she could still go out on the prairie. "But not after today," she said. "Too bad it was the last time."

She said it to make me smile and I did, but only on the outside.

I didn't ask how she knew about our move. Likely she'd heard wind of it, for nothing that goes on in the Fort stays secret for long. Aunt's face at Supper last night was proof enough that something was afoot. And she scolds *me* for showing my feelings too openly.

Sunday, September 2nd

I have been thinking of Nokum and how much I will miss her. When she came to live with the Home Guard Cree after Mother died I was only three and, since then, I have been closer to her than to anyone. Thank Heaven Father did not mind my spending so much time with her — as long as I obeyed Aunt Grace in all other matters. But before she got here, oh, those wonderful years — being cared for by Suzanne's *maman* and treated as one of the family, visiting Nokum and, when Father was home, having him all to myself. No wonder I did not take to Aunt Grace!

If she had had her way, Father would have been like most of the other officers — Lizzie's father, for instance. Poor Lizzie cannot take a single step outside the stockade. If Father had been like that, I may never have known my grandmother or her relatives, or Suzanne's aunt and cousins — at least the ones who are with the Home Guard and not following the buffalo.

Nokum says she came back because of her aching bones, but I think it was because of me. That will make it even harder for me to go away.

Tuesday, September 4th

I was walking to the dining hall with Aunt Grace and she was talking about Mr. Kennedy's many virtues — his good-natured and easy manner, his kindness, his ability to make her laugh and his likeness to my father. "Not in looks," she says, "but in personality."

She then surprised me by saying something personal. She said she would have preferred a husband of some rank within the Company — a Clerk or a Chief Trader like Father — but "Fate would have it otherwise." And though a blacksmith is not an officer and cannot be considered a gentleman, Mr. Kennedy is a skilled tradesman and his rank is above that of a common worker, or what the Company calls a servant or *engagé* — and she hopes I am not disappointed, or feel that Father would have disapproved.

I assured her that that was not the case, that even if Father had cared, he would still have been happy for her. (Tho' given the number of officers he introduced to Aunt Grace over the years, he may well have been disappointed.) As for me — *tête de cheval* — it is the *last* thing I care about!

Aunt Grace must have felt relieved to express her feelings, having no women friends to confide in, because later on she brought up the subject again. She said that in all likelihood, my father *would* have disapproved, but had he lived, she may not have been drawn to Mr. Kennedy in the first place. "He's the only one who can make me laugh the way Robbie did," she said.

I was honoured that she had confided in me, but glad that she did not go on any longer, for what do I know about such things? Except that she's right about Father. He could have made a porcupine laugh.

Wednesday, September 5th

The Wedding Day!

Aunt Grace is now Mrs. Kennedy, and Mr. Kennedy (who I am to call Uncle Rory) has moved into our quarters.

Mr. Rowand married them since there isn't a Protestant missionary now that Rev. Rundle has gone back to England, only Father Thibault at the Catholic mission, and Aunt was in no mind to wait for a minister of her liking. They signed a contract promising to have the marriage performed by a clergyman at the first available opportunity, so maybe we'll have another wedding at Fort Colvile.

Mr. Kennedy — I mean Uncle Rory — must have been relieved that the ceremony was short and to the point. He was nervous enough! He can shoe a cantankerous horse with his eyes closed, but when it came to the ring (a simple gold band from the Company Store), and putting it on Aunt's finger, he could scarcely hold his hand steady.

Once the ring was in place, the hall was cleared for

dancing. The fiddler played jigs and reels and everyone had a grand time (and a dram of rum, thanks to Uncle Rory), but no one looked as happy as my radiant aunt.

Mon dieu! I cannot believe I described Aunt Grace as *radiant*.

Friday, September 7th

Evening

Have just returned from a walk with Suzanne. We talked about my move to Fort Colvile — a six-week journey from here — and I told her what Uncle Rory told Aunt Grace and me, that Fort Colvile used to be in the Columbia District, but the border got settled between the United States and British Territory and now Fort Colvile is in the United States.

Suzanne pouted and said, "I don't care where it is, it's still too far away."

I wish she were coming so we could share the Adventure, and she said the same. I made her promise to write with news of the Fort and especially of Nokum, but she hates reading and writing, even in French, and as for English! Aunt Grace tried to teach her (and so did I) but *mon dieu*, it was hopeless. So I reminded her that since the mail does not go out very often, her promise would not be very hard to keep. And if she really had trouble, she could ask Lizzie to help her.

In return, she made me promise to write *short* letters *en français* with *simple* words so that reading them would not be a chore, either for her or for Lizzie, since Lizzie would end up helping no matter what.

We talked about Aunt Grace's lessons, and how she used to scold Suzanne, saying that teaching her was worse than skinning a buffalo. (Not that she would ever dream of doing such a thing.) We had a good laugh about that. To be fair, it was good of Aunt to teach Suzanne on occasion. She did so for my sake, I think, since her lessons were only for the officers' children.

Suzanne is lucky. She has so many friends and cousins, plus eight brothers and sisters, I don't think she'll miss me as much as I will miss her. Who will I have for a friend at Fort Colvile? No one like Suzanne. We are as close as twins, being only five weeks apart.

I am less thrilled about the move than I was at first, torn between feelings of excitement and dread.

Saturday, September 8th

It is but three days since Uncle Rory has moved out of the men's bunkhouse and into our quarters. He is such a big, hearty, boisterous fellow, he engulfs our small room. His laughter shakes the walls, and as for his snoring! It is akin to the snorting of buffalo!

I do not complain, however, for he is kind and good-natured and the nights are not long. During the day he works at the smithy and takes his meals with the men, the same as always, and spends the evenings strolling on the prairie with his radiant bride.

Will I be radiant on my wedding day? Will I be as fussy as Aunt Grace in my choice of husband? Perhaps, if he is homely or bowlegged, but I would not mind a dashing *canadien* like one of Suzanne's brothers, provided he takes me on his Adventures.

Tuesday, September 11th

Suzanne and I walked out on the prairie today — a little farther than usual, since it will be my last time. We are leaving with a small party on Saturday.

We saw a herd of buffalo in the distance — the dust from their hooves rising above the plain — and we lay down on the grass and imagined we could feel the earth shaking, the way we could when we were little, when the herds were hundreds of times bigger. Right then it hit me, that it has been almost a year since Father died, a week's journey from home. I mentioned this to Suzanne, and she told me how angry she'd been with her *papa* that day, the way he'd rushed back to the Fort ahead of the brigade and pushed right past her to speak to me. And how dreadful she'd felt afterwards, when she learned that he'd come to tell me about Father's accident.

How clearly I remember that day. The moment Papa Jacques told me the news, I felt as though I'd fallen through a crack in the ice — one minute the ice was solid, and I was looking forward to Father's return. The next minute, the ice had given way and I was drowning. Aunt Grace told me that "time would heal my wounds." I did not believe her, but she was right — at least the hurt is a little less sharp than before.

"Your *papa* was brave," Suzanne said, and it's true. Brave and adventurous, to shoot and wound a buffalo and follow it as it dragged itself into the bush. The men who saw what happened said it was something they'd all done from time to time. No one expected the buffalo to suddenly rear up and charge Father's horse, causing him to fall and be trampled. But I bear no grudge against the buffalo.

On the way back, Suzanne said, "Are there buffalo in Fort Colvile?"

"No," I said. "Uncle Rory says it's on the other side of the mountains."

The thought of no buffalo makes me sad.

Wednesday, September 12th

Aunt has written a packing list and has been after me to do the same, but I have already packed. Most of my clothing is in Aunt's trunk and the rest of my belongings are stowed inside Father's old carrying case, except for my Journal and writing tools. I'll put them inside his little *cassette* at the last minute, so they'll be at the top and easy to get at.

I have a different sort of list.

What I will Miss on Leaving Fort Edmonton and the Saskatchewan District:
Nokum
Suzanne (and her sisters and cousins)
Maman Thérèse and Papa Jacques
Suzanne's brothers (especially Emile and François)
Buffalo herds, large or small
Smell of pine gum and wood chips in the boat-building yard
Mr. Rowand (when he's in a happy mood)
Mr. Rowand's horse races
Spring break-up when the ice goes floating down the river and the brigades leave for York Factory, and the return of the brigades in the Fall when they're loaded with new provisions and mail (tho' Fort Col-vile will have brigades too)
Snowshoeing with Nokum to help her set traps
Sleigh-riding

My jackrabbit feelings hop between dread and excitement, excitement and dread.

Thursday, September 13th

Musket fire, the booming of cannon, voices singing with excitement — the brigade is returning from York Factory, and earlier than last year! Suzanne is getting impatient, she has been calling and calling, *Viens vite, toi! C'est Papa et mes frères!* So I must hurry, because it is the first time Emile and François have been with the brigade and I cannot wait to see them and Papa Jacques. They will have stories to tell! And if not, they will invent them, the way Father used to do! Why didn't Aunt Grace scold *him* for Exagger

All right, Suzanne! *Je viens!*

Friday, September 14th

Nokum and I went for a last walk on the prairie — a last walk together, I mean, for naturally she said it would be her last. I told her how glad I was that she had come back to live at the Fort when she did. Otherwise I might never have known her. What would I have done, if I had not been able to talk to her, or hear her stories, or walk with her on the prairie? All these things I told Nokum today.

She gave me a small bag of pemmican for my journey. The bag is the same as the brigade sacks, made of buffalo hide with the hair on the outside, but much smaller than the usual ones that hold 90 pounds of pemmican. She told me I could eat the pemmican whenever I wanted, or I could save it until I am as old as she is! (I know it does not spoil, but am unlikely to keep it *that* long.) She confessed in a whisper (tho' there was no one about) that she had added an *extra* handful of dried saskatoon berries to keep me in good health.

Knowing how precious *that* made the pemmican, I promised I would keep it safe and not tell a soul.

She also gave me the pouch she'd made of deer-skin as soft as the palm of her hand. It is decorated with dyed porcupine quills and smells of sage. I have never seen Nokum without it, and the fact that she would part with it made my eyes fill with tears — in spite of my effort to be strong. ("No tears," says Aunt Grace. "Crying is a self-indulgence and best done in private.")

When I reminded Nokum that I wasn't leaving until tomorrow, she said that now was the time for goodbyes because her "sore old bones" would not get her up early enough to see me off.

I began to laugh, as she is always up before dawn, but then — I could not help it — I threw myself into her arms, my throat choking with sobs, and begged her to come with me.

She sat me down, held me and rocked me like a

baby, chanting a song that calmed me a little, though I did not understand the words.

Later, as we were returning to the Fort, she explained that she could not go with me. The place is too far from her home and her family, her sister is ailing, there are children of her nieces' children who need her, and the journey would be long and difficult. She was old and tired of travelling, she said — she did enough of that when she was following the buffalo. It was time for her to stay and for me to go.

"It is your journey," she told me, and I was not to be sad, for her thoughts would always be with me.

She had been speaking calmly, to keep from upsetting me further, I think, but her voice started to break on her last few words and I could bear it no longer. So I gave her a fierce and final hug and ran through the gate to the Fort.

Fort Assiniboine, on the Athabasca River
Thursday, September 20th

A new post! A new river! *Et enfin,* the chance to record my Adventure thus far in the last of the evening light. So I must not waste words or stray off the track.

A good thing my Journal was at the *top* of a load, for if it had been at the bottom, I would not have bothered. I remember asking Father once if I could accompany him on a brigade and he said no, women and children passengers were thought to be annoyances, and the custom of families travelling with the men was no longer allowed unless —

Mon dieu, I am off the track already!

So to begin. We left Saturday morning with the usual fiery sendoff of muskets and cannon and hearty but tearful farewells. Everyone gathered in the yard to see us off — except for Suzanne (but I later knew the reason). Saying goodbye to my second family — Maman Thérèse and Papa Jacques and Suzanne's brothers and sisters — well it took the longest time, because they each demanded a hug. My ribs were sorely (but pleasantly) crushed. And then they gave me a farewell gift — a *ceinture fléchée* that has been on so many journeys, they said it would keep me safe. Oh, *quelle surprise magnifique!* I hugged my *ceinture* and wrapped it around my waist — four times, for it is very long!

"But Papa Jacques," I said, "what will you do without it?"

He assured me that he had other ones, and Emile and François each had their own, and so did Suzanne and it was her idea from the start. She could not have thought of anything more special.

Besides Aunt and Uncle and me, there are two Clerks travelling with us — one going to a post west of the Rocky Mountains and the other going all the way to Fort Vancouver — and over a dozen men who set up camp, hunt for fresh meat, tend to the horses, handle the boats on the rivers, etc. And there are a great number of horses to carry our baggage and provisions.

I did not see Nokum when we left the Fort, but a short time later I spotted her on top of a grassy slope with Suzanne and a few of her relatives. I was relieved that she was not alone.

They called out their farewells — Suzanne's voice rising above the rest — and I waved my *ceinture* and called back until they were out of sight.

The best part of the journey, and the *worst* — because I am *so sore* — was that we were on horses. Father was given one of the Fort's horses and sometimes took me for a ride, but never for an entire day. Oh . . . my poor mistreated sitting-bones!

Aunt Grace agrees with me on the *worst* part, and her groans have been equal to my own. I feel stiff and sore in muscles I never knew I had. Seeing how we staggered about, moaning and grimacing whenever we got off the horses, well it must have amused the men, though they were too polite to say anything. Uncle Rory assured us that it would get easier, and it did, but only a little, and not until after the fourth day. By then we were too numb to feel *anything*.

As for the route itself, we had prairie for the first couple of days, then squelchy muddy swamps, then dense woods with branches that whipped out to catch us off guard. It was new to me, so I ignored my discomfort as best I could and was endlessly exclaiming or pointing out trees or squirrels or birds (mostly geese), until Aunt Grace told me that I was growing tiresome, and that even the horses needed some quiet now and then.

We stop at the end of each day and the men set up camp and prepare Supper. Roast goose the last three nights, thanks to the men's shooting, and oh, the delicious pleasure of eating by a campfire in the wilderness under a darkening sky!

Uncle Rory sets up a small tent for the three of us — I would rather take the buffalo robe outside and sleep under the stars, but Aunt says the nights are cold and dangerous. One night I was awakened by the howling of wolves! I confess to being frightened (and glad of Uncle's snoring, thinking it would keep a wolf away), but what would an Adventure be without a little trembling? And now that I think of it, without sore muscles? So, Jenna, *no more groaning!*

Fort Assiniboine is much smaller than Fort Edmonton, more of a post than a Fort, but it's warm and tonight we sleep inside.

Oh, I am weary. Tomorrow we leave the horses and go by boat to somewhere else and that is all.

Jasper House on the Athabasca River
Monday, October 15th

Boats and tracking, boats and tracking, sometimes no tracking, just boats. Thank goodness we are done with the Athabasca River! Twenty-six days of going upriver — a gruelling expedition, for whenever the water level was low or there was a strong current we had to get out of the boats to lighten the load so that the men (including Uncle Rory, who is one of the strongest) could attach lines and *pull* the boats through the water. *Tracking* they call it, an arduous task! Arduous for us too, because when they were tracking we had to walk.

In truth, I did not mind the walking, for it was something to *do* and kept me warm — a better alternative than sitting with Aunt in the middle of the boat, getting wet and cold from the river splashing up and the rain falling down — which it did for three days — and afraid to move a muscle for fear the boat might overturn.

I felt a bit feverish about halfway through the journey and had some bad coughing spells, but did not want to annoy the men by moaning too loudly. Besides, it seemed churlish to moan when the men were sometimes tracking waist-deep in water.

Aunt surprised me by letting me indulge in self-pity — I was careful not to overdo it — and she did not seem to mind when Uncle Rory gave me the odd sip of brandy to ease my cough and help me sleep. He told jokes and stories to take my mind off my misery and, when I was feeling better (after a week or so) he told me that Mr. Rowand maintained that anyone who wasn't dead after three days' sickness had not been not sick at all! After a few days I felt better.

We followed the same routine each day — travelled upriver, stopped and made camp, ate Supper by the fire, listened to the men talk about their adventures on the brigades, and went to sleep in our little tent, bundled up in blankets and buffalo robes.

What else do I recall?
Days of rain and low-lying cloud or mist
Thick forests of pine
A mother grizzly bear and two cubs foraging along the riverbank
Mountain sheep with enormous horns that spiral backwards from the top of their head
Some tumultuous rapids that would have been thrilling had we been going downriver
A delicious moose Supper — one of the men shot it last week and, as it was too heavy to take with us, we stopped and camped on the spot.

The *best* part of the river journey was seeing the Rocky Mountains! At the first sighting everyone burst out with loud hurrahs, and now we are *in* the mountains — they are all around, wherever we look, like magnificent castles or fortresses towering into the heavens — so high that when I look up at their snow-capped peaks I wonder how they can still be part of the Earth — especially when all but the very tip-top is hidden by mist and cloud.

I love having Father's *cassette*. Whenever I open it I imagine him doing the same on one of his journeys. It smells of old leather, pipe tobacco, wood smoke, horses, forests — thousands of miles of *his* travels and now, some of my own. I like to imagine that he is making the journey with me.

My mother is too, I just realized, for I have her moccasins in my *cassette*, and Nokum's pouch. My whole family is with me! And thanks to Suzanne and my *ceinture*, I have my second family with me too.

Tuesday, October 16th

I have but a few minutes before we set off on the next stage of our journey — a climb to the summit of the Athabasca Pass! I have assured Aunt and Uncle and anyone who asks that I am much better and ready for the challenge.

I like Jasper House because of the mountains. It is a small post with a log house and two other buildings and the man in charge is Mr. Frazer. The house has two rooms — one for Mr. Frazer and his family (a Cree wife and nine children), and the other room is for everyone else — men who are travelling through, men who work at the post and their wives, etc. Last night Aunt and I slept with the Frazers. The children are very friendly and I spent most of the night giggling with the older girls.

Mr. Frazer travelled across the whole HBCo territory with his bagpipes as Governor Simpson's personal Highland Piper, and last night he gave us a demonstration. My ears are still hurting! I've heard the piper at Fort Edmonton many a time, but to hear the pipes in small quarters — oh, what an eerie, ear-splitting sound! The poor dogs howled and howled — I think the very mountains trembled.

We had a fine feast of roasted mountain sheep — Must put this away for it is time to go.

Boat Encampment
Wednesday, October 24th

We made it over the Athabasca Pass!

I am toasting (with tea) the men from Fort Vancouver who came up the Columbia to greet us, bringing the boats that will take us downriver. They had a crackling blaze of a fire waiting to warm us up and they had a good hot soup bubbling in the pot (made from pork and corn that they brought from Fort Vancouver). Not only that, they brought cheese, sugar, tea and a very large ham! It was not long before we were merrily feasting — the cold, wet miseries of the river crossings forgotten.

Now I must record the mountain journey before I fall asleep.

We left Jasper House the morning of the 16th and crossed the Athabasca River in small canoes. The men from our party and an Indian guide from Jasper House were waiting with horses — they had swum the horses over earlier that morning — so we mounted and set off on the route. My muscles braced themselves, for I have not been on a horse since Fort Assiniboine, and sure enough, they yelped with complaint.

The route took us through dark forests, up cliffs, over crags, and tho' each step took us closer to the summit, it also took us into colder temperatures and thinner air. Aunt and I had a little trouble breathing. Sometimes we saw mountain goats — shaggy white animals with little beards and black hoofs polished to a shine (or so it appeared). Such curious animals, leaping from one narrow ledge to another to stare down upon us. How I envied their sure-footedness!

After six days, when we were *almost* at the summit, the snow became too deep for the horses so the guide took them back to Jasper and we continued on snowshoes. Aunt Grace has always found it awkward to walk on snowshoes and fell several times into deep soft snow. Once she looked as though she'd like to *stay* there, she was so exhausted, but Uncle Rory soon had her moving again and managed to coax a weary smile.

He helped me too, at times, but though I was as tired as everyone else I didn't mind the snowshoeing. It made me think of Nokum and the times she took me snowshoeing, the two of us walking like birds on the top of the snow.

There was a small lake at the summit that the men call the "Committee's Punch Bowl," because many years ago when Governor Simpson reached the summit, he drank a toast to the honour of the HBCo and its London Committee and gave the lake its name. From that day on it has been a tradition, so we all had a sip of brandy and toasted the HBCo. I felt like a true Adventurer!

Uncle Rory (who is very knowledgeable) told me that that little lake, no more than a mile around, is the source of two mighty rivers — the Columbia River on the west side of the mountains and the Athabasca River on the east. I can hardly believe it, especially now that I see how mighty the Columbia truly is.

We had two nights of *winter* camping, whereby the men cut down pine trees, strip them of their branches and lay them on the snow to make a bed. They also make a floor of green logs and light a fire. I loved the experience of sleeping under the stars on those cold clear nights, listening to the sounds of streams and waterfalls — not yet frozen — and every part of me warm and snug except for the tip of my nose. I was relieved that the sky remained clear so we did not wake up buried in snow.

Coming down from the summit took us only five hours. It was very steep, but breathing was easier and we could remove our snowshoes.

There was no rest at the base of the mountain for then we had to cross a river — the Portage River, someone called it, and I would like to forget it. We had to cross not once but several times in freezing water and through a fast current and sometimes the water was up to the men's shoulders! Uncle and one of the men carried Aunt across and the two Clerks carried me. I decided I did not need to have the Adventure of crossing on my own and besides, I was too tired and cold and hungry (like everyone else) to protest.

Now I am warm and full. But too tired to write another word.

Thursday, October 25th

We have just been told that a small bag of pemmican has been stolen from our party's provisions. A *special* bag, containing saskatoon berries. Thank goodness mine is inside my *cassette* —

Is it? I had better look.

Later

My pemmican is safe. The *stolen* pemmican was found in one of the men's bags and Uncle Rory was called upon to punish the thief. He did so in the way of the brigades, by repeatedly knocking the man down.

I moved away and didn't watch when the punishment began, but I could not feel sorry for the culprit. If provisions are stolen, *everyone* suffers.

I just remembered — a few days ago I told Uncle Rory and Aunt Grace how I was travelling with my whole family inside my *cassette* and Uncle Rory says, "Good thing your aunt's still on her feet — your case is overcrowded as it is."

"Barely on her feet," says Aunt Grace.

Uncle Rory did some more teasing about the "brigade" in my *cassette* and made us laugh — especially when he tried to figure out where and how *he* might fit inside — and later Aunt told me that she often imagined the same as me, that "dear Robbie" was on the journey with us.

Monday, October 29th

The journey down the Columbia was spectacular. Three hours after leaving Boat Encampment we had to shoot the Dalles de Mort, deadly rapids where the river leaps between towering rock cliffs and crags for 3 whole miles. It was so thrilling my heart very nearly stopped beating! I was tempted to close my eyes like Aunt did — for to see how close the boat came to the cliffs was terrifying — but I did not want to miss a thing!

Oh, how I would love to describe my journey to Nokum!

After the excitement of the Dalles de Mort we had five days with no tracking, no climbing, no rain or snow, a fairly clear run downstream with the current. Oh, I have a mind to stay on the river all the way to the Pacific Ocean! Then I could cross the Ocean, and what an Adventure —

But there I go again, off the track.

Tonight is the last time we camp before we reach Fort Colvile, according to the men who have been this way before, and they have told me that tomorrow we will pass through the Little Dalle. They say it is not as terrifying as Dalles de Mort but has a great many dangerous whirlpools!

Fort Colvile

Saturday, November 3rd

At last our journey has ended!

We arrived here last night in time for Supper, but I had little appetite. I was still trembling after the excitement of the whirlpools (for they *were* dangerous) and tired after a long portage up and over a hill to get around some falls. The men had to carry the boats.

Mr. Anderson, the Chief Trader at Fort Colvile, met us and showed us our quarters. I went straight to bed and fell asleep.

The ringing of the morning bell woke me up and at first I thought I was home in Fort Edmonton.

Then I heard the sound of a waterfall and remembered last night's portage. The waterfall sounds very close. I think it is time to explore!

Later

I have made a new friend! Her name is Eliza and she is 12, like me, and Mr. Anderson is her father. She has a brother called James who is 8 and many other brothers and sisters.

Monday, November 5th

Fort Colvile is large compared to the other posts on our route, and has a stockade and bastions like Fort Edmonton, and horses. Yesterday I sat behind Eliza on her horse and she gave me a tour of the Fort and the farm. I was afraid that the horse-riding parts of me might complain, but they were no trouble at all.

There are acres of wheat and oats and corn as well as pastures for the cattle, and all around are high hills and mountains. Eliza showed me the mill and the dairy and the pen where the pigs are kept. She calls them "grunters," and told me that the Fort raises them for ham and bacon.

I asked Eliza about the waterfall and she told me it is not one waterfall, but several. The name is Kettle Falls and we're only a mile or so above them. No wonder we can hear them so clearly! I desperately wanted to see them but Eliza said no, as it was starting to rain.

There are not many people here, not like in Fort Edmonton, but Eliza says Fort Colvile is on the route between the interior posts and Fort Vancouver, so people pass through at different times.

P.S. Aunt Grace is so smitten with Uncle Rory that sometimes I think she has forgotten me. So tonight I put her to a test. I took my *ceinture* and wrapped it around and around my head with the fringes flapping over my face. She could not help but see it — but she never said a word. Whenever I glanced up she was working at her embroidery and smiling to herself. She's *still* smiling to herself!

I'll put her to another test another time. Right now I might as well be invisible.

Tuesday, November 6th

Now that we have settled in, Aunt Grace has been asked to give reading and writing lessons to some of the officers' wives and their children, and to teach them the ways of the British, like she did at Fort Edmonton.

The men from our party have been resting here these last three days, but this morning they continued their journey to Fort Vancouver. We saw them off and wished them well.

Wednesday, November 7th

I wrote a letter to Suzanne today and told her how much I miss her and Nokum. It was difficult describing my journey to Fort Colvile using simple words and sentences, but somehow I managed to keep my promise. I wrote in English though, so Lizzie will have to help her. I hope they can read my tiny writing, for I did not want to waste a single bit of paper.

I gave the letter to Mr. Anderson and he assures me it will get to her eventually. And if Suzanne writes back (as she promised) her letter will eventually come to me — *mon dieu,* it could be the fall of 1850, a whole *year,* before I hear news of Nokum! I always knew this about the mail, but knowing is different than *feeling,* and she and Suzanne are so far away. I must think of them often and pray that my thoughts will travel across the mountains.

Thursday, November 8th

I have just sat down — Aunt Grace has put the kettle on for tea — and said, "I found this Journal with Father's things."

"Dear, dear Robbie," she said.

"Was it wrong for me to keep it?" I asked her straight out, and added, "I suppose it was a Misdemeanor, seeing as how it was Father's."

"What's that, Jenna?" she said, looking over at

me. "I'm sorry, I wasn't listening . . . "

She wasn't listening! Not even when I said Misdemeanor! I hope she hasn't had some sort of seizure. Is this what happens when a person gets married? Well, if she has lost *some* of her senses, they must have been the hard, bad-tempered ones. I only wish she would notice me now and then.

Goodness, have I taken leave of my senses? I cannot believe I wrote that.

Friday, November 9th

Uncle Rory is not an officer so we are not as well off as before and our sleeping quarters are smaller — which makes Uncle's snoring even *more* noticeable. Last night the snorts turned into the honks of geese!

His snoring never bothered me on the brigade trail, but I was so dead weary by the end of the day I could have slept through a stampede of snorting buffalo.

He seems to like working as a blacksmith, but I have heard Aunt Grace urging him to put in for a promotion to Junior Clerk, being good with numbers. She urges in a sweet, gentle way, not in the bossy manner I'm used to.

Sweet urgings or not, Uncle Rory has not been moved. "All in good time," he says. I think it is his way of saying, "Never."

We have had several days of rain and miserable weather, but today was fine, so I rode to Kettle Falls with Eliza and James. Mr. Anderson came with us.

The Falls are exceedingly close — and the sight and sound are spectacular! They fall some 30 or 40 feet by my reckoning, in a series of cascades, into the mouths of huge hollowed-out rocks that look like giant kettles.

James said I should see it in the summer and early fall when the salmon come to lay their eggs — why, the river is so thick you cannot throw a stick in the water without hitting a salmon. And they leap up the falls!

I laughed, certain he was joking, but Eliza and Mr. Anderson said it was true, for the salmon must get up the river to the place where they were hatched in order to lay their eggs. Then they die, and the place stinks of rotting fish.

The whole business is called spawning and it happens every year, beginning in the summer. The river is teeming not only with fish, James said, but with Indians, bears, eagles, etc. etc. — all catching, trapping, spearing or feasting on the salmon.

It was starting to sound like the aftermath of a buffalo hunt.

Monday, November 12th

Eliza and James spend part of each day doing lessons (at their father's insistence) and I have been joining them. When I am not doing vocabulary exercises or parsing sentences, Aunt lets me help the younger children with their reading. I love reading and writing and am longing to advance further. If only I had some new books! I will ask Mr. Anderson if he has any books or newspapers I might borrow. Most officers have some of their own — at least they did in the posts near Fort Edmonton. They would often lend them out to people in other posts.

Outside of lessons, Aunt Grace seems to be losing interest in my education. Last night I asked her to read over a story I had written, and she did, but not in her usual way. Why, when she handed it back this morning there was not a single correction, even though I had misspelled some words *deliberately!* And tho' she said my story was "excellent," I'm not sure if she actually read it.

Next time I'll write utter gibberish — and in a messy hand! That should get her attention.

Friday, November 16th

Aunt Grace seems to like Eliza and often mentions that she is pleased I have a friend my own age. It's odd that she should say that, because Suzanne is exactly my age and Aunt Grace never took to her. Sometimes she would call Suzanne "a wild wee savage." (And call me the same.)

Eliza is the sort of "young lady" Aunt Grace was teaching the girls at Fort Edmonton to be — virtuous, polite, obedient (like Lizzie) — and Suzanne and I *did* behave that way, but when we were away from Aunt Grace and the officers' daughters and in the company of Suzanne's brothers and cousins, I suppose we were wilder than we should have been. Oh, *mon dieu,* Aunt's outrage the time she caught us having a spitting contest with the boys, and when we canoed across the river without permission, and when we snuck up to the second floor of Mr. Rowand's house to spy on the officers — oh, how I miss Suzanne!

Aunt Grace must have felt odd at first, being the only white woman in the district. Would she have come if she had known? Did Father tell her? One of these days I will ask her, as long as I'm not invisible at the time.

She might have missed having a friend. But she never tried to learn Cree and spoke only a little French, and though she was polite towards the other women, she was never very friendly. In fact she acted quite uppity and superior, even towards my nokum and Maman Thérèse. Perhaps because they were not white or only part white? Or not educated and did not take to books? (I am happy that she likes books, for that is something we assuredly have in common.)

Come to think of it, Aunt Grace is friendlier to the women here, but I think that has more to do with Uncle Rory than anything else. Some days she is like a new person.

Tête de mouton, how did I get onto this track? This is supposed to be an *Adventure* Journal, not a book of thoughts and wonderings and "maybes." I could just ask Aunt Grace about this or that, but it is more amusing to speculate. Is *speculation* a Misdemeanor? I forget.

Sunday, November 18th

I cannot stop myself from writing about another thought I've had — in the past three months I have seen more of Uncle Rory than I ever saw of Father during a similar time period, what with him travelling once a year between Fort Edmonton and York Factory. That took him away for five or six months, there and back, with time spent at York Factory and at various Forts along the way. Off he'd go in the spring and back he'd come in the fall. Sometimes he'd go on short journeys in the winter on Company matters. Did I ever have a long stretch of time with him? Of course it's the same for everyone whose fathers go with the brigades . . .

Oh, dear. I feel sad now, thinking of fathers, remembering the winter nights when Father was home and I was little, sitting on his lap as he taught me to read . . .

Uncle Rory will not go off with the spring brigade, for there is always work to do in the smithy.

Later

Tonight at Supper I asked Aunt Grace what it was like in the Orkney Islands where she and Father grew up.

She answered the same as always, that life was hard. So I said, "Is that why you came to Rupert's Land?"

"No, I came to meet Mr. Kennedy." We both laughed when she said that. "But before that, I came because you were without a mother, and my dear brother asked me to come and take care of you."

Of course there was more to it, and she told me a few things I hadn't known before. When Father first asked for permission to bring out Aunt Grace, the Company said no, because white women were not allowed. (So she did know ahead of time that there were no other white women here.) Father begged the higher-ups to give their consent anyway. Fortunately for him (but not for me), a number of senior officers had already been asking that a respectable woman be sent out to teach their daughters, and the Company finally gave Aunt Grace permission.

It was three years before she got to Fort Edmonton, what with the slowness of the mail and the long journey, and by that time I was almost 7. "You were headstrong and stubborn even then," she said, "and none too pleased at being separated from Suzanne and her family."

I wanted to know how she remembered my being "none too pleased," but by then Supper was over and she was in a hurry to meet Uncle Rory.

I remember kicking and wailing and pulling her hair! No wonder I did not take to her, tearing me away from Suzanne's family.

Thursday, November 22nd

I told a lie today (a grave Misdemeanor, but no one need know).

Eliza was wondering how my parents met. I told her that Father had gone hunting alone and been thrown from his horse and had broken his leg, and when his horse returned to the Fort, my mother was the first to gallop off and find him. She saved his life and he married her.

The *story* is true, but it happened to *Mr. Rowand* and his wife, not to my mother and father. *Everyone* at Fort Edmonton knows the Rowand story. I wish my parents had met in such a romantic and adventurous way, but Father simply met my mother at a Cree camp and that was that. He could have met her at a Fort, I suppose, if her father hadn't abandoned

Nokum and gone back to England when my mother was only a baby. I'm glad Nokum had her family to go back to.

I don't know exactly how my parents met, but I know they were married *à la façon du pays,* the way the Cree women and Company men married in the old days. It was very simple — the man asked the woman's consent, then her parents' consent, and if they said yes, the man had to pay something, like a horse or a pile of Trade Goods, and they smoked the Sacred Pipe to seal the bond.

When that ceremony was over they went to the Fort and he married her in the British way. (I suppose it would have been a civil ceremony, like the one Aunt Grace and Uncle Rory had.) My mother must have looked doubly radiant that day, since she was married twice.

Saturday, November 24th

The weather is exceedingly cold but it has not yet snowed.

Friday, November 30th

All week I have been thinking about Fort Edmonton, especially Nokum and Suzanne, wondering how they are faring and if they miss me as much as I miss them.

Last night I asked Aunt Grace and Uncle Rory if they missed Fort Edmonton, and Uncle Rory gave such a vigorous laugh I was taken aback. Had I said something funny? No, he explained, it was the thought of missing "old One-Pound-One and his temper" that made him laugh. "No one'd miss that," he says. "He was a jolly sort when he wanted to be, but that temper of his kept getting worse."

"Only because his limp was worse and he was in pain," said Aunt Grace, coming to Mr. Rowand's defence.

Hearing Uncle Rory use Mr. Rowand's nickname brings back the rhythm of his lopsided step — a good warning when Suzanne and I were spying, and we heard it on a wooden floor. Then we knew it was time to flee.

Friday, December 7th

Cold and rainy.

Saturday, December 8th

I have been thinking of our journey to Fort Colvile and how thrilling it was, compared to staying in one place day after day. No wonder the brigades are so excited when it comes time to leave the Fort, especially after being bound there all winter, for it was not only the start of spring but the start of a new

Adventure. That's how it seems to me, though I could be wrong, now that I have seen first-hand how hard they have to work.

I am a little disappointed that we did not have a *real* Adventure on our journey. We were not kidnapped by hostile tribes and rescued by brave Heroes, for instance, and we did not witness an act of heroism, like an Indian fending off a grizzly attack or Uncle Rory saving Aunt Grace from drowning when our boat overturned, *if* our boat had overturned. But the mountains and rivers and rapids were magnificent.

Last night I opened my bag of pemmican and had a nibble before going to sleep. The smell of fat and meat and berries, the taste on my tongue . . . it took me so close to Nokum I could almost hear her voice. Oh my, the tears are welling up as I write. (Here comes Aunt Grace. Will she notice, and ask why?)

Later

Bedtime. I had a little more pemmican to cheer me up.

Aunt Grace did not notice I was crying. I expect I would have to commit a Misdemeanor of the Gravest Sort to get her attention.

Wednesday, December 12th

Yesterday the temperature dropped and it started to snow. It has not stopped snowing. It reminds me of going into the woods with Nokum to set animal traps. The quiet swish of our snowshoes.

Saturday, December 15th

Disappointments —

I am disappointed in Eliza, for she is not at all like Suzanne, or any of my other friends at Fort Edmonton. She does not even like my stories.

I am disappointed in my Journal entries. Of late they are nothing but thoughts and feelings (and a bit of weather). There is no harm in that — in fact I have found the recording of such things somewhat worthwhile — but I wanted my Journal to be full of Adventures. Of course I could make up my *own* adventures and write them down, but what if something exceedingly thrilling and adventurous *was* to happen and my Journal was too full to record it? That would be *crushing!*

So I have decided to put it away for a while. I will make up stories to entertain Eliza and James — well, at least James will be entertained — and concentrate more on reading the books Mr. Anderson has lent me. Even though they are dull, and mostly about Agriculture.

1850

Wednesday, June 12th

The promise of a New Adventure has prompted me to retrieve my Journal, for I may be going on another journey — not back to Fort Edmonton but to Fort Victoria. It's quite a new Fort, only 7 years old — and it has a school! A *real* school, and it is run by real teachers, a Reverend Staines and Mrs. Staines and, according to Mr. Anderson, they have a reputation for being *excellent* teachers. He is sending Eliza and James, and I desperately want to go with them — not only because of the school, but because of the journey. Nokum was right when she said I was restless. Perhaps my fate is not to remain in one place but to be always on the move — like Nokum herself, before she got too old.

I would also like to be away from Aunt Grace. Not because she is forever scolding and finding fault, like before — quite the opposite. She is so smitten with Uncle Rory that I may as well not be here at all!

Mon dieu, could I be jealous? No, but I suppose I am somewhat out of sorts after having had her undivided attention for years. Is contrariness a Misdemeanor? At least she will not object when I broach the subject of leaving. After all, I am almost 13.

Friday, June 14th

James told me that Fort Victoria is in the Colony of Vancouver's Island, an island in the Pacific Ocean, and Eliza said no, it's just a little ways off the mainland, and I said it's still in Pacific Ocean *water*, so what does it matter how much of the ocean surrounds it?

Mr. Anderson overheard us arguing and showed us on a map. So we were all right. What an Adventure, to attend school on an island where each day I would be able to see the ocean!

Eliza and James are going to travel with Mr. Anderson and the Fort Colvile brigade as far as Fort Langley, and then to Fort Victoria, and they are leaving as soon as the brigades from the smaller posts in the area arrive with their furs. If Aunt Grace gives her consent, I will go with them!

Tonight I will approach Aunt Grace. I am determined to go, and if she objects — tho' I see no reason why she would — I will stow away amongst the furs. That would *really* be an Adventure!

Sunday, June 16th

Unbeknownst to me, Mr. Anderson had already told Aunt Grace and Uncle Rory about the school, so when I brought up the subject, Aunt was prepared — with one objection after another! I should have expected it, knowing how argumentative she can be.

She said she could not manage without me and that I could read and write "exceptionally well" and *she* would continue my schooling as before. She said I would hate being confined to a schoolroom for longer hours than I have been accustomed to, and I would hate the Strict Rules — much stricter than those *she* ever imposed — "Mark my words, Jenna" — and she said that I was setting myself up for disappointment.

She had not reckoned that my stubbornness would equal her own. "Father would have encouraged me to go!" I said (though I wasn't certain about that), "and now that you're married, you will not even notice I'm gone!"

"How can you say such a thing!" she says, but before she could add another word I told her she needn't worry about the expense because I could use my inheritance to pay the subscription of a pound per month, including my board, and that I would do like the Andersons and pay until June of next year.

I know how thrifty she is and, tho' I have no experience in money matters, it must have sounded reasonable, for she did not look aghast. Besides, she knows that the money Father left for me is substantial, for he had saved all his wages over the years. Aunt credits his "Orkney spirit," but there is little to buy in a Fort, even a large one like Fort Edmonton.

In the end, she consented. She could have withheld the money, since she is my guardian and I am too young as yet to have control of it, but she is not mean-spirited at heart, especially now that she is married. I think she was willing to be convinced from the start. In fact she probably told Mr. Anderson days ago that I may go, knowing that I will be in good hands. But being contrary by nature and enjoying our verbal debates, she had to put up a fuss.

Later

Aunt Grace actually looked *hurt* when I said (somewhat peevishly) that she would not even notice I was gone. Does she not realize she has been ignoring me? Or am I guilty of Exaggeration?

No, surely not.

Saturday, June 22nd

The brigades have arrived! As soon as their fur bales have been checked and repacked we will be on our way.

Meanwhile I am helping out in the dairy, churning butter and making cheese. A pleasant change from helping Aunt Grace make soap — my hands are still red and sore from the lye.

A "slight delay," says Mr. Anderson. Some of the bales were improperly packed and now the furs must be recounted and repacked.

My Adventure continues at the butter churn.

The traders are not the only ones repacking, for I have packed, unpacked and repacked my possessions several times. A few books and my winter and summer clothing are now packed inside the small trunk that Aunt is letting me take, and I have put personal items, pencils and keepsakes (my "family" again!) into Father's *cassette*. My Journal too, but not yet.

And Aunt made me two new dresses! They're presently too long and too loose, but very pretty, and she assures me I'll grow into them before long. As well as making the new dresses, she has lowered the hems and let out the seams of my old ones. She also gave me a white handkerchief embroidered with flowers.

I am tremendously excited!

It is well past midnight but I am unable to sleep for excitement. Tomorrow I am on my way to an

Unknown Island! I have disobeyed Aunt Grace's order not to light another candle to write by, but by the time she discovers this Misdemeanor, I will be far beyond her reach. For I am not only setting off on an Adventure, I am setting off *On My Own.* (Another Misdemeanor — *Exaggeration.* "Stop stretching the truth!" Aunt would say. To her, Exaggeration is as wicked as Lying, Stealing, Talking Back, Putting on Airs, and Wasting Time, Money or Candles.)

My Misdemeanors have been accumulating lately. Is it because I am leaving that Aunt Grace is so attentive? I wish she would go back to ignoring me.

"On my own" is not a *real* exaggeration. It simply means that I am setting off without Aunt Grace. It does not mean I am blazing through the wilderness alone. The distance is too great and I do not know the way.

She would also berate me for "Unknown Island," since Vancouver's Island is not unknown. But it is unknown to me. As of tomorrow I will be facing a multitude of Unknowns, but am I setting off with Trepidation and Sadness? No! And if I were, I would not admit it since it was my idea in the first place.

Now that I am almost on my way, I can put into words what I have been thinking in secret for months. My mission is to write a Novel — not now, in this Journal, but one day. Aunt Grace would knock me down for Pride, Arrogance, Conceit and any number of Misdemeanors, but I hereby confess that my recently retrieved Adventure Journal is but a prelude to my Major Work.

If I were writing a Novel, I would call the first chapter *In which Jenna Sinclair sets off on an Adventure to an Unknown Island!*

My bones are clattering with anticipation. My Independent Life is about to begin.

Monday, July 1st

Here we are at last. I am not sure where here is, but we have stopped moving and are about to settle down for the night.

It took a long time to find a camping spot with enough water and fodder for the horses, but the fire is lit and everyone is occupied. Gros Ventre is preparing the evening meal, some of the *canadiens* are removing the packs from the horses — tents and bedding, baggage, provisions and furs — others are pitching tents, feeding the horses, gathering firewood, etc. Eliza is writing in her Journal and James has wandered off.

We left Fort Colvile this morning at dawn. Aunt Grace cried at my departure and I could not help but do the same — tho' I tried not to — for there is no telling when we might see each other again. Uncle Rory gave me a beaded necklace from the Trade Store and a great bear hug.

When I looked back and could no longer see

them, I felt an unexpected ache of loneliness. The feeling could well have stayed with me had it not been for Lafleur, our scout, who unwittingly banished *all* feelings except for sheer terror, for he was suddenly galloping *towards* us, waving his arms and shrieking.

Was it an Indian attack! Was my Adventure to be over on the first day?

No, for the men were hooting with laughter, particularly Mr. Anderson. Knowing that Lafleur is terrified of snakes, he had killed a big rattler below Kettle Falls and hung it on a bush some ways ahead of his scout. Lafleur reached the spot, came face to face with what he thought was a live rattlesnake and rode back in a panic.

Eliza told her father that the next time he decides to play a practical joke, he has to warn us in advance.

We saw no Indians today, and the closest thing to a *real* terror are the mosquitoes — they are biting us senseless.

Too dark to write, and the smoke from the fire is stinging my eyes. As soon as I have eaten I am off to bed.

Several days later (I have lost track of time)

The Daily Routine on this journey is the same as on the one from Fort Edmonton to Fort Colvile.
"Dehout! Dehout!" The wake-up call at dawn.

Loud, stretched-out yawns, grunts, sighs, groans, but up we get. If not, the tent is collapsed on top of you — like this morning, when a group did not move fast enough. Their scrambling under the canvas gave everyone a good laugh.

Once everyone is up, the men load the horses and the day's ride begins. Fortunately I was able to go riding a little at Fort Colvile, so I'm not as sore as I might have been.

About eight in the morning, we stop at a convenient spot for Breakfast. The men are busy unpacking, laying the cloth, boiling and frying, eating and drinking and smoking their pipes. After that, while the repacking is being done, some of the men wash and shave — but only the hardiest because the river water is very cold.

They all carry a razor, a towel and a bit of soap in their pocket, though some have not put these items to good use. (Nor, in truth, have I — the towel and soap, I mean.)

If there is no pool with still water to use as a mirror, they rely on Eliza and me to give our opinion. Some of the *canadiens* have even asked us to wield the razor but we have refused. I would never be able to keep my hand steady at such a task and I would hate to be responsible for giving someone the nickname Pas de Nez!

The other morning James told Gros Ventre that his moustache was too long — first on one side, then on the other — and the poor man shaved most of it off trying to make it even. James and I found this hilarious, until Gros Ventre threatened to shave off our heads! (I think he meant *hair*.)

An hour for our Breakfast stop and we are off again.

Dinner is about one o'clock, and is always a cold meal of pemmican, so no fire is needed and we stop but twenty minutes, about the time it takes for the men to smoke a pipe or two.

I told everyone that I'd had a hand in making the pemmican, since Fort Edmonton supplies all the brigades, and Lafleur said he thought it tasted especially good. His words made me happy. (Eliza told me later that he was flirting, and that I should not encourage him by smiling.)

Onward we go until it is time to set up camp. Then we have Supper.

The men smoke their pipes and tell stories around the fire, swatting at blackflies and mosquitoes. I am usually too tired to do anything but sleep.

Another Camp

As of today we have trekked across country to the Similkameen River and followed the Similkameen to the Cascade Mountains. (Mr. Anderson told me the names so I could record them.) There was still snow in the mountains and we saw a number of mountain sheep. After crossing the mountains we came to the Coquihalla River. We will follow it all the way to Fort Hope, where the Coquihalla flows into Fraser's River.

Our first night on the Coquihalla, James dared me to wash in the river. I pretended it was no worse than any other river, though I could scarcely breathe for the cold. My fingers are still numb. From now on my face and hands can stay as dirty as everyone else's.

Coquihalla. Similkameen. I love those names, the way they flow like the rivers.

Another Camp — and the Worst

A few words in haste —

We are packing up and leaving earlier than usual to escape the mosquitoes. The air is black with them! I spent the entire night swatting, scratching, scratching, swatting, *crying* with the torment — I even have bites in my mouth and throat. I wanted to throw myself into the Coquihalla.

Fort Hope, on Fraser's River

We arrived here two hours ago. Fort Langley has been expecting our brigade and sent canoes to Fort Hope to take us down Fraser's River. Tonight we are resting here.

This morning we saw an Indian *swimming* across the Coquihalla — probably to escape the mosquitoes. His clothing was tied in a bundle on top of his head.

When we stopped for Breakfast, James and I dared each other to wade barefoot into the water and see who could stay in the longest. I lasted seven seconds. James won by a hair with no end of gloating.

Eliza is too much of a lady to play such games and rolls her eyes in disapproval. I had hoped we would become better friends on this journey, but I prefer James's company, perhaps because he is daring and a mischievous little scamp.

The men are taking pains to wash and shave. Many are plunging into the river in their breeches and soaping themselves from head to toe. There is a great deal of splashing and larking about. Tom-foolery, Aunt Grace would say. And what would she say if she had heard me call out, *"Attention,* Lafleur! *Y'a un serpent!"* In two leaps he was out of the water!

(Eliza will accuse *me* of flirting this time.)

Must close — Gros Ventre has asked if his beard needs more trimming. He now knows better than to ask James.

Fort Langley
Wednesday, July 17th

Tonight we are sleeping in Mr. Yale's house. He's the Chief Trader of Fort Langley, so it is comfortable

— tho' I enjoyed sleeping in a tent.

We started at 4 o'clock this morning. The *canadiens* were dressed in their finest (and cleanest) clothing — deerskin breeches and embroidered jackets, moccasins decorated with beadwork, ribbons fluttering from their caps, *ceintures fléchées* tied 'round their waists, the long fringed ends swinging as they loaded the canoes.

I loved when the fur brigades arrived at Fort Edmonton, but the excitement of seeing them cannot compare to the thrill of travelling with a brigade — my heart leaping with the rhythm of the paddles, the gusty, rollicking, familiar songs. The experience left me breathless!

As we drew closer to the Fort, the *canadiens* lashed the canoes together and allowed them to drift downstream. The songs turned to whoops and cheers and the men fired muskets into the air. Up ahead I could see the HBCo flag rising to the top of the flagpole and we knew what was coming. "Plug your ears!" I cried, as the first cannon was fired. The welcoming roar echoed far and wide.

Father used to say that the arrival of the fur brigades marked the end of winter — reason enough for celebration. This time their arrival takes me one step closer to Fort Victoria and school —

Oh. And one step farther from home.

I am suddenly overcome with sadness. The excitement over the brigades, the entire ritual — it is so familiar, but what wouldn't I give to have Nokum and Suzanne here to share it, and dear, dear Father.

Thursday, July 18th

Brigades have been arriving from the Interior with no end of cannon fire and celebration. Some even got here on Tuesday, before we did. What's more, the Chief Factor of Fort Victoria, a Mr. Douglas, is coming to meet the fur brigades. He is expected any day now, which has the Fort in a feverish state of excitement, for he is not only the Chief Factor of Fort Victoria, but of the entire Columbia District. I hope he is a kindly sort, for Eliza, James and I will be travelling to Fort Victoria under his care. Mr. Anderson and Mr. Douglas made the arrangement some time ago, since Mr. Anderson has to return to his duties at Fort Colvile.

James and Eliza have been looking more and more unhappy since our arrival here, knowing that they will soon be apart from their father. I would like to cheer them up, but what can I say? I know the feeling too well, and it is not easily shaken by words.

Friday, July 19th

I was watching one of the brigades unloading their furs and a dashing *canadien* smiled at me. I must have turned the colour of his *ceinture*, my face felt so hot, and all I could think to do was walk away. I hope I smiled back. It would have been rude not to.

Eliza happened to be going by at the time and told me it was unseemly to flirt. She talks such nonsense.

Saturday, July 20th

A *sailing* ship is anchored in front of the Fort! What would Nokum say? No doubt she would be as awestruck as I was, watching the ship as it glided up the river like a magnificent white bird.

The ship is called the *Cadboro*. It looks enormous to me, but I have heard that it is only "a small schooner," used for carrying trade goods up and down the coast.

Mr. Douglas was on board, and his arrival was marked with stupendous roars of cannon. A launch took him from the ship to the jetty, and then it went back for the other passengers.

Now that I have seen Mr. Douglas, I am a little anxious about the rest of my journey. He looks exceedingly stern and formidable. His very height is formidable! There will be no practical jokes on the way to Fort Victoria, and I daresay he will not tolerate the slightest Misdemeanor. (But I could be mistaken.)

I would like to see him alongside Mr. Rowand.

Tho' they are both Chief Factors of large districts, they could not appear more different — the one tall, thin, stern and glowery, the other short, fat and jolly with a handsome dimple in his chin. Of course Mr. Rowand was not always jolly — Uncle Rory jokes about his temper, and Father once said that Mr. Rowand could halt a rebellion with his temper alone! Mr. Douglas could probably do the same.

Later

I was wrong. Mr. Douglas *looks* stern, but he has a kind nature. Eliza and James think so too, for when Mr. Anderson introduced us, Mr. Douglas greeted us warmly and showed a great deal of interest in the journey we had made. He even said he was looking forward to taking us to Fort Victoria.

Sunday, July 21st

Last night after Supper there was dancing in Bachelors' Hall and everyone was there, even the children, and the men were asking the women and girls to dance reels, and Jean-Pierre, the one who smiled at me yesterday, invited me — not once, but twice!

There is so much going on — furs loaded onto the ship, provisions taken off, provisions repacked and loaded into canoes for the first part of the brigades' return to the Interior, and I watch and wait and wait and watch, silently urging them to hasten before I die of impatience.

I have written a long letter to Aunt Grace, and Mr. Anderson says he will give it to her when he gets back to Fort Colvile. I have also written another letter to Suzanne. Mr. Anderson is taking it, too, and will put it in the mail packet marked for the Saskatchewan District. He says it will go with whoever happens to be travelling up the Columbia and crossing the Rockies, like someone going to a new post, or a small party returning home after taking leather goods to Fort Vancouver, or someone carrying mail from the Columbia District to the east. I imagine it making a journey like the one I made from Fort Edmonton — going from post to post, on one route or another, down rivers, up rivers, across the Rocky Mountains — and eventually it will reach Fort Edmonton and end up in Suzanne's hands, whereupon she will clasp it to her chest and shed tears of joy on hearing from her absent friend. By then I will be in Fort Victoria and, if Suzanne keeps her promise, come Fall I will receive a letter from her! And will clasp it to my chest and shed tears, etc.

I've just had some pemmican. Many of the people here know one another, from other brigades or Forts in the Columbia District, and the Andersons have friends who were passengers on the *Cadboro*. There are a lot of children here, like Aurelia and Bella Yale, for instance, and everyone is friendly enough, but I feel a bit lonely.

I will feel better once we continue our journey.

Thursday, July 25th

Au revoir, Jean-Pierre! The brigades left with their provisions this morning and tomorrow we leave Fort Langley.

My Adventure will continue at sea!

Friday, July 26th

We left Fort Langley this morning in canoes — huge dugout canoes manned by Indians from Fort Victoria. Eliza and I were in one, with Mr. Douglas, and James was in the other. The river widened and branched off in many directions, and as we got closer to the sea I could smell the tang of salt water. The *Cadboro* had left well before us and was waiting at the mouth of Fraser's River — and there the water changed colour, from the silty brown of the river to the blue of the sea.

I saw what appeared to be an island and said,

"Is that Vancouver's Island?"

Mr. Douglas said no, it was just one of the many small islands in the strait between the mainland and Vancouver's Island. He pointed to a range of high mountains, hazy in the distance, and said *that* was Vancouver's Island, and we were making for the southeast tip.

The island looks enormous!

We are now on board the *Cadboro* and tonight we are sleeping in hammocks. My stomach already feels queasy with the rocking of the ship — even tho' it is at anchor — and my writing is getting wobbly so I will stop for now.

Saturday, July 27th

Land! It does not pitch or roll!

I am sitting in the shade of a magnificent maple at a place called Point Roberts, where the canoes were forced to land a few moments ago. My stomach was exceedingly thankful.

We left the *Cadboro* this a.m. and reboarded the canoes, after a night of hammock-rolling and mosquito-swatting. It is a wonder I didn't roll out of the hammock altogether! It was thrilling to be on the sea and away from the river, each stroke of the paddles taking us farther from the mainland, but the thrill did not last, for the wind began to whip the sea into mountains and valleys! It was a terrifying experience to be in the canoe as it rode to the peak of one wave, only to plunge nose down into the dip before the next one. Up and down, so far down I could not see *above* the oncoming wave and feared I might never see land again, let alone touch it.

We put to land before I lost my Breakfast, but Eliza was not so fortunate.

The men have set up camp and we are staying here until the wind dies down. I hope it will take some time, but if I am to live on an island, I suppose I will have to get used to rough water. Facing a tumultuous sea will be part of the Adventure, like facing a blizzard or an ice storm at home. No matter what the conditions, an adventurer must have courage and fortitude.

I can use my sea experience as part of my Novel!

"Heave, ho!" Captain Jean-Pierre hollers. "A storm of immense proportions is surging towards our gallant vessel and our lives are in perilous danger . . . "

James has come to sit beside me, looking glum. He was climbing a maple tree and fell. Mr. Douglas was greatly alarmed — he rushed over to help James get up and to make sure he wasn't hurt. (He wasn't.)

I am glad James did not dare me to follow, for I would have done so. The branches look very inviting.

A short time ago James asked what I was writing. I told him I was writing an account of my adventurous journey as practice for writing a Novel.

"Am I in it?" he says.

"Do you want to be?"

"Yes!" he says.

"Well that's good, because you already are."

I read out the bits about him and he was pleased, except for the tree part.

"Change it so I don't fall," he says.

I promised I would change it in the Novel itself, but not now, because now I have to record the facts truthfully. In the *real* Novel I can make changes.

"So if there are people you don't like," James says, "you can make something bad happen to them."

I had not thought of that until he mentioned it, but he is right. I can do anything I want in my Novel. I could even use a real person as a model for the Hero or the Villain.

List of Potential Villains
No one, except for Aunt Grace when she was cross

List of Potential Heroes and Heroines
Father
Jenna
Suzanne
maybe Jean-Pierre

Land again, and almost time for Breakfast. This time we are on a small pebbly beach. I'm close to the fire, wrapped in a wooly HBCo blanket and trying to get warm.

We left Point Roberts yesterday evening while it was still light. The wind had died down but there was still the odd whitecap skipping along the waves. It was a pretty sight, and the sunset was glorious.

Eliza and I were curled up on mats in the centre of the canoe, and when it started to get dark we were given blankets to make up a bed. It was cozy and warm — and adventurous, spending the night on the water — and I fell asleep listening to the splash of paddles and the paddlers' songs. They sing to the rhythm of the paddles like the *canadiens* do, but *their* songs sound more adventurous — even fierce, to my mind, as if the paddlers were warning the sea that if it dared to stir up the waves they would be ready! I felt content and safe and not a bit queasy.

Just before dawn I awoke and discovered I was drenched and the canoe was taking on water. The wind was blowing a gale, howling over our heads. The paddlers were yelling, one man bailing as fast as the water poured in. Eliza cried for her father and I was anxious for fear my journey might come to an untimely end. At the same time, I found the experience wildly adventurous.

Even more exciting was when one of the men took a blanket and made a sail! With that we rode the waves at tremendous speed and made straight for land.

Last night before I fell asleep I saw something mysterious. With each stroke of the paddles a strange silvery glow appeared, like a cauldron of stars, a sky turned upside-down. I do not know the cause but it was truly a wondrous sight.

Mr. Douglas told me that our paddlers are "Songhees." They come from a village near Fort Victoria. I spoke to one in Cree but he did not understand — and told me so in English. It was broken English mixed in with some of his own language, so it was a little hard to follow, but I made sense of it all the same. It was foolish to think he would know Cree away out here, for even the Plains Indians have different languages.

Now it is time for Breakfast, and a long rest before we set off again.

Monday, July 29th

Today is my 13th birthday! I told the others, and they wished me a happy birthday, which cheered me up for a while, but I'm feeling sad again. It's the first birthday I've spent away from Fort Edmonton and, not being with my family and friends, and with the land and sea and air so different — there's too much missing for a birthday. Even the *smell* is different here, especially when the tide is out, like now. Eugh! It's like fishy, salty mud.

We are on land again, this time for Supper. The sea is much calmer. Tonight we will sleep in the canoe and tomorrow we will reach Fort Victoria!

Tuesday, July 30th

At last I am in Fort Victoria on Vancouver's Island! Presently seated at a small writing table in the girls' dormitory, on the upper floor of Bachelors' Hall. Eliza and James were taken to Mr. Douglas's house and the other school boarders are elsewhere and I will be meeting them shortly. Meanwhile, I have "my new home" to myself. Mrs. Staines (who runs the school with her husband) gave me a few moments to "freshen up" before Tea, but there is precious little water for washing, and I must record the end of my Travel Adventure before my School Adventure begins.

My introduction to Vancouver's Island was a wet one, thanks to Eliza. She splashed me to wake me up! I yelped with the shock, for the water was icy cold. And as James's canoe was drawing up alongside ours, we woke him up the same way, and he splashed us back!

Our water fight might have continued had not Mr. Douglas interrupted. "Clover Point," he said, indicating the grassy point of land we were passing. He told us he had stepped ashore on that point seven years earlier, while searching for a site to build a new Pacific Fort, and had walked over fields knee-deep in red clover and wild grasses.

A short time later he drew our attention to a hill whose slopes ended at rocky cliffs dropping to the sea. "That's Beacon Hill," he said. "A short walk from the Fort."

The hill is impressive, but the beacon is no more than an empty barrel on top of a pole. Mr. Douglas said its purpose is to warn ships of a dangerous rocky ledge that remains underwater even at low tide.

We passed several crane-like birds, greyish-blue in colour, standing or wading in the shallows. They moved gingerly, raising and lowering one long leg at a time, as if they did not like getting their feet wet. James called them herons and said they were fishing. They did not seem bothered when we paddled by.

Nor did the seals! There were dozens of them, playing and basking on a rocky island not far from shore.

It was a beautiful morning for our arrival. Clear sky, sparkly sea, white-peaked mountains across the strait to our left, and on our right, the coast of Vancouver's Island.

Eventually we entered a narrow passage bordered

by dense green forest. It was fortunate the Songhees knew where they were going, for I would have kept paddling and missed the entrance.

Before we knew it we had rounded a point, and there was the harbour. A *gigantic* ship was at anchor — a hundred times bigger than the *Cadboro* — and standing like a sentinel above the harbour was my new home, Fort Victoria — its HBCo flag snapping in the breeze and the men firing

Oh, *mon dieu,* I almost forgot. Time for Tea!

Later

I have disgraced myself and learned my first lesson. When Mrs. Staines tells you to freshen up you must do so, no matter how little water there is.

I made it to Tea *barely* on time, but when I presented myself in the school's dining room, Mrs. Staines took one look at my face, hands and fingernails and growled, "This will not do."

I fled upstairs and scrubbed up as best I could. Mrs. Staines looked me over a second time and allowed me to stay, tho' grudgingly. Thank goodness I even *remembered* the Tea. Had I appeared late as well as unwashed, I might have been locked in the Bastion.

So, to continue where I left off.

The men fired up the cannon to welcome Mr.

Douglas and we went ashore. We had to climb an embankment to reach the Fort and I was looking here, there, *everywhere,* instead of watching my step, so I stumbled and fell onto the path. The Kanaka carrying my *cassette* and trunk helped me up. (I have learned that there are many Kanakas working here. They come from the Sandwich Islands — in the Pacific Ocean but farther south — where the HBCo ships go to trade.)

A man with a pale face and big moustache greeted Mr. Douglas in the Fort yard, tho' neither looked overly keen to see the other. His name is Mr. Blanshard, and he is the Governor of the Colony.

There were many children about, eyeing the "newcomers," no doubt wondering who was who and what we would be like, but I had no time to eye them, for Mrs. Staines whisked me up to the dormitory. I *did* have a chance to eye her — a raven with its feathers fluffed out. But fluffed out crisp, black and shiny, with not a feather out of place.

One of the girls, Lucy, gave me a sympathetic smile at Tea, when I was sent back to wash, and even rolled her eyes in Mrs. Staines's direction, as if to say, Don't take it too hard, we have all been in the same situation.

Everyone was friendly at Tea, the girls and boys who are boarding at the School, and we were all introduced but I have forgotten half the names.

Lucy has been a pupil here for months and knows

a lot about the place. She told me that the big ship in the harbour is the *Norman Morison,* the Home Ship. It left London last October, sailed around Cape Horn at the tip of South America, then headed up the coast to Fort Victoria. It arrived here in March with a year's supply of goods. No wonder it is so huge! I expect the Home Ship in Hudson's Bay is the same. Father used to describe how big it was, but I could never picture it until now.

I just remembered something curious. When we were paddling into the harbour I spotted an enclosure a little ways from the Songhees village (which is across the water from the Fort). There were four animals inside that looked so white and woolly I thought they were sheep. Well Mr. Douglas explained that they are actually a type of dog, but are shorn like sheep, and their hair is woven into blankets.

Eliza and I thought he was teasing and started to laugh, but he assured us that what he said was true. What's more, he told us that the wool dogs are so valuable they are kept on a nearby island, well away from the other dogs, and we were lucky to have seen any at all that close to the village. (They might have been ill or about to have puppies.) We heard them too — a high-pitched howl that sounded more like coyotes than regular dogs.

The trees here are gigantic, taller and wider than any I have seen, and they are *everywhere,* even in the

Fort yard — six massive oaks, one of which James has already tried to climb. (He was not successful, but at least he did not fall.)

Wednesday, July 31st

My first full day at Fort Victoria is almost over. I have found a cool spot beside the Bastion wall and will stay here until the mosquitoes drive me indoors. (Are there any prisoners in the Bastion? In my Novel I could help one escape!)

After Breakfast Lucy showed me around the Fort. I tried to take in all the details so I could write about it, but Lucy is such a talker I doubt if I can remember the half of it.

We started by climbing upstairs to the Gallery — the one at the northwest corner of the Fort. A rare treat, for normally we are not permitted, but this time Mr. Douglas gave us permission.

Oh, what a spectacular experience, looking over the top of the stockade! The mountains across the strait, the entrance to the harbour, the Songhees village across the harbour, James Bay (the name of the bay near the Fort), a salmon house on the beach, the long inlet flowing to the north — Lucy called it the "Arm" and said it was a fine place for an outing — and rolling hills in the west. And in the east, all on its own, an enormous, cone-shaped, snow-covered mountain called Mount Baker, which Lucy said was a volcano that could erupt anytime! (I could put that in my Novel!)

And there's a deep ravine close by with a cemetery on the edge and an inviting little bay where the ravine meets the harbour and where the boys like to go bathing — well, I was so taken by the splendour of my new surroundings I did a bit of a jig, which made Lucy and the watchman laugh. (But not unkindly.)

Then the watchman took us to the Gallery in the southeast corner. Lucy pointed out the Company gardens directly outside the Fort and next to them, Reverend Staines's garden where he grows his "prized lettuce" and other vegetables. Lucy said that the boys have to weed and thin out the plants and her brother Alec (who's also at the School) hates it. There are more Company gardens farther out to the east and also to the south on the other side of the Bay. And a very large farm called North Dairy Farm to the north where they have sheep as well as cows, and a smaller dairy close to the Fort where we get our milk.

Lucy pointed out the start of a trail that goes around James Bay to Beacon Hill and said the class sometimes goes there for Nature Studies and picnics — oh, I cannot wait to explore!

The northeast and southwest corners are 8-sided bastions with openings in the top for the cannon and rifles.

After we came down from the Gallery, Lucy whisked me around the yard, pointing out belfry, bunkhouses, Trade Store, Company Store, storehouse for furs, blacksmith's shop — where the smithy, Mr. Beauchamp, fires up the marbles that the boys make out of clay — and the buildings where Mr. Douglas and his family live and where Mr. Finlayson and his family live and the quarters where the workers and their families live — my goodness, there was a lot to take in for such a small Fort.

What else? Oh, a stable for horses outside the stockade and a barn, a pigsty, a bakery, and more than that I cannot remember. But I will know well enough before long.

The upper floor of Bachelors' Hall has the girls' dormitory and the boys' dormitory. The lower floor has the teachers' quarters and a room where we have lessons *and* meals (so I will call it the School and Dining Room to make it sound grand).

The quarters for the unmarried officers take up the largest part of Bachelors' Hall. There is a large Common Room in the centre and two rooms on either side, each with its own door, where the men sleep. I hope they don't snore as vigorously as Uncle Rory.

It is a novelty, eating in a room with only the other boarders and Mrs. Staines. The other children at the Fort take their meals in the dining hall with the women, same as usual. (I looked inside the dining hall and it is very plain, not grand like the one in Fort Edmonton with its painted walls and gilt scrolls.) A Mr. Field and his wife serve our meals.

My bed is made of boards and there are HBCo blankets for the mattress and covers. Just like always. The only difference is the woven cedar mat placed over the boards — similar to the ones we had on the canoes. I like the smell of the cedar. Lucy says the people on the coast weave the inner bark of cedar trees and use it for almost everything, even hats and cloaks.

The dormitory walls have no covering, not even tarpaper, so there are only the logs to keep us from the night air. Mosquitoes and rats — and there seem to be a great many of those — get in through the cracks. Last night as I was settling into bed I saw an enormous rat running along the stovepipe. (The stove will not be lit until the fall, says Lucy, no matter how chilly the nights.)

We share a washstand and a bucket of water for washing, but can only use a small amount. Lucy says there will be more in the rainy season. The only fresh water is from a well in the yard and it dries up in the summer — there are no streams running nearby. The water has an odd taste and looks cloudy. Lucy says it is because of the clay in the ground.

We have tallow candles that must be extinguished by 9:00, and there is a chamber pot under each bed.

Lucy is 13, the same age as me. The rest of the girl

boarders are between 6 and 19. Eliza will be moving into the dormitory tomorrow. For the time being she and James are staying with Mr. Douglas and his family. He has a wife and five daughters.

Even though Mr. Douglas is a Chief Factor and is in charge of the Columbia District, he does not have a grand house like Mr. Rowand's. He does not even have a house! His living quarters and his office are in the same building as the dining hall.

Governor Blanshard does not have a house either. He is waiting for his house to be built. In the meantime, he has to live with Mr. Douglas. He is not happy about it, says Lucy. No wonder! I should think a Governor would have his own house.

Lucy knows so much about everything partly because she has been here since February, and partly because she is a snoop. She told me so herself! (I did not tell her that snooping was a Misdemeanor and that I have been scolded for it on many occasions.)

Before we put out our candles last night, she showed me a loose floorboard. It is between our two beds, and when you lift it up you can see what is happening in the Common Room. A Spy Hole! How perfect for my Novel! The boys have a Spy Hole too, she says, but ours is better. No wonder she likes to snoop!

The best part of last night was hearing the familiar call of the watchman after he had closed and locked the gates. *O-h-e-s W-e-e-l-l* . . .

Aunt Grace used to grumble, "Why can't he say 'All's well' and be done with it." I like the long drawn-out comfort of the words.

Time to go in. I am weary of swatting mosquitoes.

Thursday, August 1st

My first day at Staines School.

First, Mrs. Staines had to inspect my person.

Hands, face and fingernails clean?

Yes, scrubbed to the bone.

Hair brushed and groomed?

Yes, double-brushed and braided so tightly it made my scalp twitch.

Next, she inspected my clothing. She told me that my moccasins were acceptable, as was my dress, but where was my hat? When I told her I never wore a hat, she gave me a white bonnet that looks like a coal scuttle. I am to wear the bonnet at all times, like the other girls, to keep the sun off my face. For my skin has been "bronzed by the sun to a most unsightly shade." (Her very words.)

After that she gave us a test on how well we could read and write and do sums. Later on she asked about our other accomplishments. I wanted to mention all the things I could do well — set traps, walk on snowshoes, speak Cree, make moccasins, dye porcupine quills, do beadwork, make pemmican, etc. — but no sooner had I started than she flapped her arms and said, "No, no, I meant *accomplishments.* Can you draw or paint? Can you dance or sing?"

Dance or sing? "Of course," I said, thinking it a foolish question. Whereupon she ordered me to sing a hymn.

"Do you know 'Rock of Ages'?" she said.

"It's my favourite!" I said, pleased beyond belief that she had chosen that particular hymn. But I did not sing it mournfully, the way Rev. Rundle had liked it, but in a lively manner — so lively, in fact, that when James started clapping to the beat, the others were quick to join in.

Well, Mrs. Staines would have none of that. She ordered me to stop and turned her attention to James and Eliza. They sang the same hymn but fared better than I did, for they kept the tone serious.

I am going to be singing many hymns, because Mrs. Staines says her "young ladies" (as she calls us) have to lead the hymns in Service. That is on Sunday. And every Saturday afternoon "the young ladies" have a class in Deportment.

There goes the bell, and the dogs are barking and howling just as they did at home. Must hurry and wash before Supper.

Later

Some of the girls must think they are quite the grand ladies, for they were snickering behind my back as we were going into our dining room. I overheard the girl they call Maggie say that my dress looked like a bag with holes cut in for the neck and the arms, and that it was horribly out of fashion. I whirled around and snapped, "I don't care about fashion!" My reaction shocked them into silence.

But I was so angry, I could not stop there. "My aunt makes my clothes and I do not like to hear her work being ridiculed. And she made this dress especially for School so I would have something new, and I like it, and if my dresses were good enough for Fort Edmonton and Fort Colvile, they're good enough for here."

At that point Mrs. Staines appeared and we sat down to Supper.

What is fashion, anyway? Besides being something that the dress and I are "out of."

All I know is that *beaver* hats were once the fashion and now silk hats are the fashion. Father used to grumble about the HBCo coffers not being as richly filled because now the "toffs" in Europe were putting silk on their heads instead of fur. Well, if fashion means putting a coal scuttle on my head, I am better off without it.

What use is fashion in Fort Edmonton or here? If Father had lived he might have ordered me a "fashionable" dress (one that didn't look like a bag), but Aunt Grace would never have considered it, not even for herself. Caring for one's appearance is a sinful mix of Pride and Vanity, as well as a waste of money, especially when you have to order 12 months into the future, and by the time the ship arrives with your dress you might be smaller or larger than you thought you would be. So better to spend the money on oatmeal.

I missed Fort Edmonton's oatmeal porridge this morning. Breakfast here is tea without milk, and bread with sticky black treacle. But Lucy says we have jam sometimes. Dinner so far has been salmon, coarse bread and potatoes, and Supper was much the same.

I wish I were back in Fort Edmonton.

List of possible Villains for my Novel:
Mrs. Staines
The girls who were making fun of me

Friday, August 2nd

The day began with a vigorous scrubbing of hands and plaiting of hair. (My skin and scalp still smart.) Then — to prove that I did not care about fashion or what anyone said about my clothing — I put on my prized *ceinture fléchée*, tied it proudly around my waist and marched in for Breakfast. Maggie and her friend Sarah said the sash looked silly with a dress and Lucy asked where I had beached my canoe. Everyone laughed but I held my head higher and sipped my tea.

Sarah and Maggie are now on my list of Villains, but I did not object to Lucy's remark (although it was meant to poke fun at me). The *ceinture* makes me feel Adventurous and Brave, able to suffer the most torturous hardships when on a brigade — and compared to *that,* a little teasing is of no account. James said my *ceinture* looked dashing. Mrs. Staines took one look and raised her raven-feathered brows, but said nothing.

James looked wretched in his school clothes — leather breeches and a moleskin shirt with buttons the size of dinner plates. I caught him looking at my sash with envy.

We sat in our "uniforms," girls on one side, boys on the other, waiting on tenterhooks as Mrs. Staines made her inspection, and when she commented on our cleanliness and well-groomed appearance — such relief! I swear our collective "whews" could be heard across the yard.

Later in the morning Mrs. Staines remarked on my Reading, Composition, Penmanship and Mathematics skills. She said I must have had "a superior tutor."

"Only my aunt and my father," I said proudly. I added that my aunt had gone to Fort Edmonton to instruct the girls with special permission from the HBCo and at the request of my father and other officers — even Mr. Rowand the Chief Factor. And that though she was not formally educated, she was extremely well read and had insisted I work hard at my studies and read for two hours every day. And that was *after* her lessons. But I did not mind for I too love to read. (I did not tell Mrs. Staines that there were times I hated Aunt for it, usually when the day was hot and my friends were larking about by the river, or when I wanted to help Nokum make moccasins or dye porcupine quills.)

Mrs. Staines raised her brows with surprise. "Whatever did you find to read?"

An easy question! *The Pilgrim's Progress,* the Bible, *Johnson's Dictionary of the English Language, Oliver Twist* and *Nicholas Nickleby* by Charles Dickens — books that Father and Aunt had brought with them or had ordered from London. I also read whatever newspapers the brigades brought from the Home Ship, even if the news was six months old. Aunt would make me read out loud and would question me on the meanings of words, and we would talk at length about the subject matter.

By then Mrs. Staines was smiling. (Yes, *smiling.*) "You say you read *Johnson's Dictionary?*"

"Not cover to cover," I admitted.

"My word!" She turned to the class and said, "Let that be a lesson to the rest of you."

My classmates were not smiling. I noticed a few scowls and fancied several arrows aiming in my direction.

In the afternoon Rev. Staines took over the class.

He turned out to be a more deserving target of scowls, etc. and *my* arrows (with poisoned tips) were quick to join the others'. He is a brute! If he sees you fidget or squirm or blink the wrong way or yawn or smile (but why would you), sneeze or pass wind or scrunch up your brow in confusion — Heaven help you! His switch is always in hand and he is more than eager to use it. One of my mosquito bites was begging to be scratched and I had to oblige — only to hear the whistling of air as the switch came down. The backs of my knuckles are still stinging.

A new Villain for my Novel: Rev. Staines. I will change his appearance, though, and give him one eye, like the wicked schoolmaster Mr. Squeers in *Nicholas Nickelby.*

When Rev. Staines wasn't whipping someone, he was teaching. It might have been History. He speaks with a mouthful of pebbles and the words roll around so slowly and ponderously, one loses the meaning before he is halfway through the sentence. And just when you think you *might* understand, he has swallowed a new bushel of pebbles and is rolling them out on another topic.

As for my fellow pupils, there are 27 in all, 17 girls and 10 boys. 4 of the girls are too old to be my friends — the oldest is 19 — and 10 are too young. Annie is the youngest, about 6.

One of the boys is Mrs. S's nephew, Horace. He is about the same age as James and comes from

France. The youngest boy is 6 or 7. He is a tough little beggar who tags along with Alec and Davy, the two oldest boys. They call him Radish. Another little scamp is Thomas.

Most of the pupils are between the ages of 12 and 14, and half of them are girls, like Eliza, Lucy, Maggie and Sarah (Thomas's sister) and Jane Douglas.

There are only 3 of us — 2 boys and me — who do not have a brother or sister at school. 4 of the Douglas girls are here (the 5th is too young), and 6 children from the Work family (5 girls and a boy).

Only the children of HBCo officers or ship captains can attend Staines School. The other children are mostly *canadiens* and Roman Catholics, and go to their own school. It is in a small log building just outside the Fort. I have seen their teacher, Father Lempfrit. He looks kinder than Rev. Staines.

Some of the pupils have had some learning, from missionaries or the odd teacher, but most have not, and appear to be far behind in their Reading, Composition, Penmanship, Spelling and Mathematics.

Sarah and Maggie, who laughed at my dress and *ceinture,* accused me of showing off during the lesson, since I answered more questions than anyone else, but I was not showing off on purpose. I was happy and proud that I knew so much. A double Misdemeanor, being boastful and proud, but Aunt Grace is not here to scold and I do not care what the others may think. Although I would like them to like me. Perhaps I should be a little less eager to answer questions.

I wish I could write a letter that would reach Aunt Grace or Suzanne tomorrow. No, I would be content with next month.

Saturday, August 3rd

It is only half twelve and tomorrow is *hours* away, hours that I must endure in this stifling, ratty dormitory without Dinner or Supper. And why? Because I left the Fort without permission and without telling anyone where I was going. But how could I? An Adventurer does not know in advance *where* he will have an Adventure, and part of the Adventure is the unknown and unexpected.

As for permission, I *meant* to ask — in fact I was about to ask Mrs. Staines right after Breakfast, but then I overheard Sarah and Maggie and some others making fun of my moccasins, saying they were even *more* unfashionable than my dress, the way they were decorated, but at least they matched my "ridiculous sash" and then Maggie said, "She doesn't even try to look English."

Well I flared up inside, so burning with hurt and anger I could not turn around and confront them, not this time, because they were talking about Nokum's precious gift — my mother's moccasins.

And to think I put them on this morning to make the day special.

So I ran outside to get away from the girls — I did *not* want them to see how upset I was — and I forgot about Mrs. Staines and asking permission and before I knew it I was through the gate and on the trail that goes to Beacon Hill. And the whole time I was imagining that Suzanne was with me and I was telling her what happened and saying, So they think I don't look English? Well I won't act English either, if it means being snooty like them — and soon enough I realized I was halfway around the Bay.

Well, there was no point in turning around *then,* and I was back in time for Dinner, so where was the harm? No harm at all, but a cause for war — Mrs. Staines marching into the dormitory as I'm washing my hands, *demanding* to know where I've been — and exploding when I say, "Are we not allowed to explore?"

"EXPLORE??"

Aunt Grace could have taken notes from the rant that followed. Mrs. Staines was *responsible* for my welfare, it was *unladylike* to go rambling in the wilderness without a companion, *anything* could have happened, the Indians were *not always to be trusted,* I had gone off without telling anyone, leaving her and Rev. Staines to worry as to my whereabouts — and on top of all that, I have the gall to be *flippant!*

"Allowed to *explore?*" she shouted. "You are a little girl!"

I could have told her about the girls' teasing and how I'd run off without thinking, but I did not want to tell tales — the girls would never like me if I did — and besides, my exploring did turn out to be an Adventure and I was glad of it, no matter the consequences.

If this were a Novel I would call this chapter *In which Jenna Inflames the Wrath of Mrs. Staines and is Unjustly Punished!*

I am too furious to go on.

Later

I have been holding Nokum's deerskin pouch and it has helped me calm down. So I will set my mind back to this morning. A bright and beautiful morning, with no lessons to spoil it — well naturally I wanted to explore beyond the Fort.

I had asked Lucy to come with me, certain that she'd be an adventurous sort, but she said Mrs. Staines would never allow it and there was no point in asking. As it turned out, there was no chance to ask anyway, so I went off on my own.

At the head of the Bay there's a little brook, and a plank that crosses it. By then I was enjoying myself, my hurt and anger were spent and, best of all, my moccasins felt as if they had been made especially for me. So I crossed the brook and on I went, through woods so dense I could see nothing but trees, mostly evergreens, and so tall I could not see their tops. It was a novelty at first — dark and mysterious, a perfect place for someone to hide — but I soon felt closed in, and was desperate for the open sky and a breeze.

By and by the path left the woods and I found myself at Beacon Hill, gazing down at the Strait of Juan de Fuca and the Olympian Range. (Yesterday's useful Geography lesson: the place names around Fort Victoria.) And spreading out from the hill, a wide-open meadow that ended in ploughed fields, which I took to be the Company's Beckley Farm. (I think that's the name Lucy mentioned.) I could have rested on the hill but I was hot from my walk and the sea breeze was so refreshing I decided to explore a bit more. As I was running down the hill I stumbled upon a trail that led me down the cliff and to a cove.

The tide was out and little fountains were spurting up all over the beach — a curious sight, and I now know the cause. They're made by clams!

Well I was watching the little fountains when two canoes turned into the cove. There were no men, only women and children, and after beaching their canoes, they took out some baskets and pointed sticks and started to dig.

I went to have a closer look and one of the boys

told me about the clams. Well not *told* exactly. He was trying to explain something, using gestures and a bit of English (like the word *clam*), and as I was standing there, trying to understand, I felt a spurt of cold water on my leg. I yelped, startled, and everyone laughed. Right away the boy dug out the culprit to show me that the clams make the fountains by spitting out water! They're cooked in a fire and when the shells open, they're ready to eat. The other children helped with that part, pointing to shells and open mouths, and rubbing their stomachs to show that clams are very tasty.

By then the sun was high and I was worried that I might be late for Dinner. So I retraced my steps and got back to the Fort just as the Dinner bell was ringing. Rushed upstairs, and was washing my hands when Mrs. Staines marched in and crushed my spirit. *Little girl?* I am 13!

I will put her in my Novel and make her suffer.

Still Later

Time: Somewhere between Dinner and Supper
Dormitory: Hot and airless
Jenna: Confined to Misery and Gloom
Visitors: None
Actual Activities: Exercises in Reading and Mathematics, writing in my Journal
Imagined Activities: Taking Mrs. Staines out on a

canoeing expedition and tipping the canoe (and not saving her)

Future Activities: Learning to paddle a canoe (a dugout canoe, like the ones the Songhees have)

Natural History Lesson: clams squirt water, etc. Also saw several herons and some odd little scuttling creatures — do not know their name, but they hide under rocks and have eyes on stalks and look like spiders.

Still Later

After writing, reading, thinking and moaning for *hours* I wanted to do something active. So I decided to look for another Spy Hole.

I got down on the floor and examined every board, every crack, every knot, starting at my end of the dormitory, and before I was halfway across — at the foot of Annie's bed and under a rag rug — I found one. My own secret Spy Hole!

It's a large knot, difficult to remove, and it looks down on one of the rooms off the Common Room. Whose room is it? There's a cot, a table, some shelves, but no personal belongings, so at the moment it must be no one's. A Clerk or some other officer will move in one day (I hope) but for now my find is a disappointment. Unless it is used for a secret rendezvous! I will keep an eye on it just in case.

Almost time for the evening chorus of bell and

dogs. I will check the knot to make sure I've replaced it securely, and then I will have some of Nokum's pemmican. It is no punishment for me to go without Supper.

Still Later

Time: After Supper
Dormitory: Pleasantly cool
Jenna: Bored and disappointed. Nothing and no one to spy on.

Oh — what I forgot to mention:

There were a lot of Songhees on the slopes and meadows on the opposite side of Beacon Hill from where the path came out. A celebration? A picnic? A working bee? A war party? They were busily engaged in *some* sort of activity, and it must have been enjoyable, for I could hear laughter. (So not a war party.) If I hadn't been so hot I would have gone in their direction and spied on them.

Even Later

Time: Bedtime
Dormitory: Noisy
Visitors: Lucy, Eliza, etc.

Everyone wanted to know about my Adventure, even Sarah and Maggie, and Lucy brought me some bread and treacle. It was kind of her to think of me, and I was tempted to tell her about my secret Spy Hole. But I didn't. She told me the scuttling spidery creatures were a type of *crab*.

Sunday, August 4th

My first Sunday at Fort Victoria.

The bell clanged for Church Service sometime after Breakfast and we trooped over to the dining hall — pupils, servants, officers, wives, children, everyone attached to the Fort.

Mr. Douglas was there with his family, and Governor Blanshard, and Lucy pointed out a few of the others — Mr. Finlayson (the Chief Trader) and his family, Mr. Durham (his assistant), Dr. Benson, Mr. Yates (a carpenter) and Mrs. Yates. All the Kanakas and servants were there, except for the *canadiens,* who attend mass with Father Lempfrit.

The air was hot and close, and Rev. S's sermon was boring. My eyelids felt heavier and heavier and it was such a struggle to keep them open I gave up trying. They closed of their own accord and dragged my head forward. Fortunately Rev. Staines did not notice.

Alec was not so lucky. He must have been hearing a tune in his head, for he started to mark time on the wooden bench. It wasn't long before Rev. Staines interrupted his sermon and shouted, "You, Mac-Gregor! Stop that devil's racket at once!"

"It's not me, Sir," says Alec. "It's my fingers."

"Insolent Boy!" Rev. Staines roars, and sentences him to a caning after the Service. No mercy, not even on Sunday.

And no more nodding off! We all sat up to attention, even the grown-ups.

The best part of the Service was standing up to sing the hymns.

I longed to spend the afternoon outside but, alas, we had to stay indoors and learn short prayers called Collects. There is one for each day of the church year, but fortunately we do not learn them all at once. There was another Service in the evening.

I thank Heaven that Sundays come but once a week, but even that is too often.

Later

I wrote a letter to Aunt Grace and Uncle Rory, telling them a bit about my journey across the strait, the School, the Fort, etc. Mostly to let them know that I arrived safely. I can hear Uncle Rory's laugh when he reads that I managed to squeeze him and Aunt inside my *cassette* to join the rest of my family, and thanked them again for the embroidered handkerchief and beaded necklace.

Rev. S's face turns the colour of puce when he is angry and the veins in his neck and on his forehead swell and throb like giant worms about to crawl out. During his Latin lesson this morning I kept my eyes on his face to see if anything interesting might happen, like a vein spouting open, but it didn't.

Eughh! Latin. *Do, das, dat, damus, datis, dant.* Forms of the verb *to give.* I give, you give, he/she/it gives, we give, you give and they give. I do not give a *damus* for Latin. Or that Parson Puce is a Classical Scholar. Or that he studied at Cambridge or some such uppity place in England. But I would give a very great deal if P.P. would stop reminding us that he is a Classical Scholar who graduated from Cambridge, etc. etc. *Das, dat, damus!*

We are also learning French. I expected to love French lessons since I already speak the language, but alas, I speak the *wrong kind*. We all do, according to Mrs. Staines. She speaks French fluently, and often switches from English to French within the same sentence, hoping to catch us off guard (my theory). She has been here a year — does she still not know that French is the working language of the Forts and that everyone speaks it?

Ah, but *her* French is Parisian French — the "proper French" — and the one we must learn. According to *Madame* Staines, our Canadian French is harsh to the ear and difficult to understand.

Well I expect her ear will get used to it, for I doubt that we will be speaking Parisian except in class. Except for Horace, who already speaks proper French, and the girls who like putting on airs. They can go to Paris for all I care.

Lucy tells me that the Rev. and Mrs. Staines were teaching in France before they came here, and Parson Puce was not even a parson. He took "holy orders" so he could receive a higher salary with the HBCo.

Oh, and Mrs. Staines scolded me for muttering to myself when I was doing my work. "Muttering?" I said, for I had not been aware of it.

"An irritating habit," she says. "That and the humming."

"Humming?"

Yes, that too was irritating.

So I apologized and promised I would try not to hum or mutter in class. It must be a habit, something I no longer notice. Did Aunt Grace ever mention it? I cannot remember.

Later

I gave the letter I wrote yesterday to Mr. Douglas, who assured me it will be put in the communications packet for Fort Colvile and go out at the soonest opportunity.

We had an earful from Rev. Staines this morning. Someone stole vegetables from his garden last night and did we know anything about it? No, we did not. Other than that, School was much the same.

At Dinner, Mrs. Staines is teaching us the Art of Conversation. None of us have had trouble talking, but now there are rules. Mrs. Staines introduces a topic, and we take turns speaking. It is part of the girls' Deportment Curriculum (Latin word of the day), but she believes the boys could benefit as well.

Today's topic was *Where we are from.*

I said I was from Fort Edmonton, the most important Fort west of York Factory, because that is where all the furs of the Prairie are stored, and all the York boats for the brigades are built, and all the pack horses are bred. I added that Fort Edmonton has a reputation of being the most dangerous and troublesome post on the Prairie because of all the fighting that goes on between the Cree and the Blackfoot.

At that point Sarah interrupted (politely) and said, "I thought you were from Fort Colvile, like Eliza and James."

I explained that Fort Colvile didn't count because I had spent only one winter there.

Then it was Lucy's turn. She said (politely) that I must be mistaken. The place she and Alec were from, Fort Rupert, was the most dangerous because two English seamen were massacred by Indians last year, and that was the reason her father had sent her and Alec to Fort Victoria.

It was not Davy's turn to speak but he jumped in (rudely) and said he had seen a massacre. We were all ears but Mrs. Staines would not let him go on. Her list of appropriate topics does not include massacres.

Davy was making it up anyway.

The Tale of the Murdered Seamen — a perfect title for my Novel! Or *Massacre in the Wilds of Fort Rupert.*

After Supper, Alec told us the story of how three seamen had deserted their ship to go after the gold in California, and one man had drowned and the other two had been shot in the heart, supposedly by Indians. Both had been stripped naked (we did not need to know that particular detail) and one had been placed upright in a hollow tree. The other man was left on the ground.

It was hardly a *massacre,* but in my Novel I could make it so, and I could change the setting to Fort Victoria and Rev. Staines could be one of the unfortunate Victims and

Mrs. Staines has just come in and given us salt to place around the wicks of our candles, saying it will make the tallow last longer. In her next breath she said it was time to blow out the candles. Fiddle!

Wednesday, August 7th

Last night I was telling Lucy more about Fort Edmonton, since she had asked, and I ended by saying that it was a more interesting place than Fort Victoria.

"What a pity you can't go back there," she says.

I told her I could if I wanted to.

"How? You have no family there. You're an orphan."

"My grandmother is there, and my second family," I said, and told her about Suzanne and Maman Thérèse and Papa Jacques.

"They don't count," says Lucy.

"What do you mean?" I said, challenging her.

She shrugged and went off.

Lucy is a puzzle. Kind one minute, hurtful the next — and for no good reason. I don't know if I trust her enough to be friends.

Maggie's blue sash has gone missing.

Thursday, August 8th

The weather is so fine, Rev. Staines has promised to take us on an outing on Saturday, provided no one misbehaves or neglects their schoolwork. He has not said where the outing will be or how we will get there.

I wish it could be on a sailing ship to the Sandwich

Islands. Our watchman, a Kanaka, told me it is a beautiful tropical place far to the south, with palm trees and an ocean as warm as a bath. It sounded like paradise! When I asked why he had traded that for Fort Victoria he said it was to make money and to see something of the world.

Of course our outing will not be to the Sandwich Islands. Besides, who would want to go all that way with Rev. Staines? Not I!

All the same, I am excited about a School Outing and will strive to be as good as all the gold in California.

Friday, August 9th

I hate Parson Puce. He might have told us at the beginning that his outing is only for the *boys*. The other girls are not bothered but I am exceedingly angry. If Suzanne were here, we would stage a rebellion.

Saturday, August 10th

After Breakfast I asked Mrs. Staines for permission to go for a walk — since the boys were about to leave on their outing. I promised I would be back before Dinner and would not go beyond Beacon Hill, and to my amazement, she said yes. (It might have been because she was distracted — two of the boys were arguing and Rev. Staines was nowhere in sight — so Mrs. Staines may not have paid much attention to what I was saying, only wanted me gone so she could attend to the boys before they came to blows.)

I wandered out to where Rev. Staines has his garden, just outside the stockade. I stopped for a minute and talked to the workers from the Company's gardens, though Mrs. Staines would have disapproved. Speaking to them and hearing their French reminds me of Suzanne's papa and the other *canadiens* at Fort Edmonton, and it is a pleasant change from speaking English. I asked one, a Mr. Minie, about some odd-looking cattle I had seen on the farm and learned that they are long-horned cattle from Spain. He told me about a Captain Grant who had come here as a settler and shot one of the cattle, mistaking it for a buffalo! (He has obviously never been on the Prairie).

Another worker asked if I had been to Beacon Hill. When I told him I had, and was going there again, he told me to "mind the Songhees," for they were digging up the meadow. "Been at it a week," he said.

He looked inclined to say more, but I thanked him and hurried off, excited about seeing the Songhees at their digging. A spy mission! And even more exciting — as I was approaching the meadow I discovered a Secret Lookout!

It is near an oak grove behind Beacon Hill, in a

sprawling cedar with low branches spread out in a circle around the trunk. The branches are so thick I could scarcely see the trunk, not until I'd crawled in underneath. And what did I discover when I reached the trunk? A ladder of branches begging to be climbed! I fancied them saying, "We've been waiting for you, Jenna!"

So up I went! From one branch to another, pausing now and then to listen to the birds and the squirrels and the rustle of wind, climbing higher and higher until I reached a comfortable perch. I sat astride, leaned against the trunk and fancied I was floating in a sky of leafy green.

I had a lovely view through gaps in the branches, and what did I see? A large party of Songhees, women and children, armed with woven sacks and pointed sticks. They were singing, chatting and laughing as if

Fiddle! There goes the bell for Dinner.

Later

So to continue with the Songhees.

It seemed to me that they were on a picnic, but instead of laying out a cloth and hamper, they were indeed digging. Whenever they came upon the dead leaves and stalks of a particular plant, they stuck in their stick to form a hole, then reached in and pulled out what looked like a small brownish onion, but in the shape of a pear — a root of some sort, which they put into their sacks. They worked in an organized way, being careful not to miss a spot. Why, it was not that different from the farm workers digging potatoes!

Other groups around Beacon Hill and beyond were engaged in the same activity and, from the little mat shelters set up here and there, I reckoned they were camping out on the meadow until the job was done. They must have been at it for a while, for I could see dozens of bulging sacks.

One of the older women reminded me of Nokum, tho' I could not see her clearly. It was the way she moved, as if her joints were aching. And at that moment I had the oddest sensation that Nokum was right there beside me. I heard her voice and saw her face — I swear I felt her hand on my shoulder! A shiver passed through me and left me happy and sad, and I feel the same now — sad because she is so far away but happy because she feels so close. Climbing down the tree was more difficult than climbing up, and my legs were shaking by the time I reached the ground. Even so, I am determined to visit my Lookout whenever I can. I will be like the beacon on top of the hill! Or maybe not, since no one will be able to see me, and what good is a beacon if it cannot be seen?

Perhaps there is another kind of beacon, one you carry inside so you do not lose your way. Nokum is my beacon. I see her face in my mind and it lightens my heart. It reminds me of who I am and where I am from.

Goodness, I'm thinking too much again. It was never so in Fort Edmonton — I was too busy *doing* to be thinking, and with Suzanne and Nokum to talk to and even Aunt Grace

I had better stop. I can hear Aunt Grace scolding me for another Misdemeanor, Self-Pity. And "there'll be none o' that, lass!"

I find it curious, the way people at Fort Victoria refer to the meadows as "the prairie." I will keep calling them *meadows* though, because "prairie" means something different to me, and I do not want my entries to be confusing.

It is almost time for our next lesson in Deportment.

Saturday Evening

How does a lady stand? How does she sit? How does she move? Smoothly, elegantly, gracefully, etc. (If Suzanne were here I would have whispered, "Carefully, if she's in a tree.") All of which are supposed to make us "good material" for a suitable marriage.

"What makes a suitable marriage?" I said.

"A suitable husband," said Mrs. Staines, and everyone laughed.

My face grew hot — not only with embarrassment but also with anger. How dare they mock me! I had asked the question in all seriousness, for no one had given thought to my marriage — not me, not Father (as far as I know) and not Aunt Grace (for her own prospects were more important). I suppose a suitable husband for me would be an Englishman of the officer class, but beyond "white" and "officer," what makes a man suitable? Mrs. Staines is married to Parson Puce (white, English and officer class), but I think her idea of a suitable husband is far different from what mine would be. (Perhaps a dashing *canadien* like Jean-Pierre or Suzanne's brother Emile, or François.)

In any case, the Deportment lesson itself was amusing. We practised walking, sitting, etc. under the watchful eye of Mrs. Staines, trying not to giggle as she swished around in her billowy skirts, her hair tightly crinkled in ringlets. She waltzes about as if she were the Queen of England.

We had some leisure time before Supper, so Lucy and Sarah and I went outside to play. We were rolling hoops when the boys came back from their outing. They looked a fright, for they had painted one another's faces with berry juice, and it had turned into a dust-streaked mess of purple and red. Puce! We teased them about it but they were actually proud of the effect.

Rev. Staines ordered them to go off and wash, but Alec, Davy and Radish lingered to tell us about their day — a long wagon ride to a farm and (stopping on the way to pick berries) a glass of fresh milk at the farm, listening to one of the farmers play his fiddle.

Sunday, August 11th

Same as last Sunday.

What would Father have said about Rev. Staines?

I overheard a conversation once, between Father and Mr. Rowand, after Rev. Rundle came to Fort Edmonton, and Mr. Rowand was saying that the missionaries were the worst thing for the Company, because all they did was keep the Indians singing hymns and praying instead of hunting and trapping. Father agreed. Rev. Staines is different. He is not a missionary and has little to do with the Songhees, as far as I can tell. He doesn't keep them from trapping or fishing, he only keeps his pupils from enjoying themselves.

Nothing happened today.

Monday, August 12th

The vegetable thief has struck again! Such a calamity — Rev. Staines is in a fury because one of his lettuce plants was stolen and he was planning on having a salad supper. We were grilled without mercy. Who would want his maggoty lettuce? It would taste as sour as his temper.

Tuesday, August 13th

Today I was yelled at five times. Once for stumbling over a Latin phrase. Once for braiding the fringes of my *ceinture fléchée* instead of keeping my hands folded on the table. Once for helping Eliza when she could not solve a problem in Mathematics. Once for giggling when Mrs. S's stomach gurgled. Once for asking Parson Puce to repeat a question because I had not heard it the first time and "Why was that, Miss Sinclair?" "Because I was not listening, Reverend Staines." "Why were you not listening?" I did not want to tell him that I was thinking of my grandmother and so I shrugged. Insolently, I suppose, because I had to stay in and write 100 lines of Latin. At least I was not scolded for humming to myself when I was doing my Spelling exercises.

I had expected that Learning would be an Adventure. I had not expected to be confined in a schoolroom, ordered about, made to sit just so, raise my hand, stand up to speak, ask permission to go to the privy, etc. I had not expected to be shouted at for asking a question or for helping someone with an answer or for daydreaming. I had not expected a real school to be as dismal as Dickens' Dotheboys Hall, or a real schoolmaster to be as cruel as Mr. Squeers — I thought the descriptions in *Nicholas Nickleby* were exaggerations! Not so, for Rev. Staines gives the boys canings or smacks or thumps on the head for the slightest Misdemeanor, and he has such a temper. We never know from one moment to the next what might set him off — what throws him into a rage on Wednesday is scarcely noticed on Friday and vice versa. Oh, I have made such a mistake in coming here. Aunt Grace would say, "I told you so," and she would be right.

But if I were to return to Fort Colvile after paying my full subscription? Oh, the grumbling! She would be too proud to ask that the unused portion of my subscription be returned, and she would complain about the waste of that money for years.

Why did I pay until the end of June? How will I survive until —

I won't survive! Not unless a new schoolmaster arrives, or a schoolmaster's assistant, like the kind and heroic Nicholas Nickleby. But I fear that will not happen.

If I were a boy, and 14, I could work in the Trade Store or in the dairy or stables, or perhaps be taken on as a Junior Clerk — but there's no use thinking of what cannot be. I am utterly forlorn and miserable and disheartened.

Veni, vidi, vici. Julius Caesar, 47 B.C. He came, he saw, he conquered. I will not be yelled at for not knowing *that* again, but there will always be something.

Reverend Staines, 1850. He came, he saw, he tormented.

Last night we were awakened by a startled screech coming from the boys' dormitory. It was followed by a great deal of banging.

It turns out that Radish discovered a rat in his bed. It was nibbling on a crust of bread that he had stowed away. He killed it by slamming it against the wall.

Rev. Staines has offered the boys one shilling for every ten rats they catch.

I wish I had a friend here like Suzanne. No one seems to like me. Is it because of my *ceinture* and old-fashioned dresses and the way I tear off the coal-scuttle hat when Mrs. Staines is not around? Because I fidget in class and sometimes hum or mutter to myself when I am thinking? Because I *think* too much? And spend a great deal of time writing in my Journal? They have made comments about *that* from time to time — not unkind comments, but things like, Whatever can you be writing about? Nothing happened, etc. (I wonder how Eliza and Maggie and the others who keep journals can write so little!)

Maybe they don't like me because I come from the prairie. Or do they think I am common? They have no reason to, for Father was a Chief Trader.

Perhaps it is because of Uncle Rory. Eliza knows him from Fort Colvile. She knows that he and Aunt Grace are my guardians, and that he is not an officer but a blacksmith, and even though he is a skilled tradesman he is only one level above a servant. By the Company's rules, he could never be considered a gentleman and, if I were *his* daughter, I could not be attending this school.

Perhaps they do not like the way I behave. The other day Mrs. Staines praised one of the older girls for being very English in her manner. Am I not English enough for the other girls? Aunt Grace taught us proper English manners and Christian values and I *do* behave properly — well except for going off and exploring, but only because I do not see the harm in it.

Perhaps they think I behave more like a worker's daughter. Before Aunt Grace came to Fort Edmonton, I did not have to follow the rules so strictly, and I was mostly with Suzanne's family or with Nokum, at least when Father was away. And besides, many of the girls from the other officers' families were too young or too old to have as friends, except for Lizzie.

Well the rules are still the same. The Officer Class does not usually mix with the Tradesmen Class or the Servant Class.

I do think too much. Why can't I make friends with the girls and stop worrying about whether or not they like me? I think — and this has only just come to me — it's because I don't know *how*. My best friends, like Suzanne, have always been *there*. And Eliza was my friend for a while, I suppose. But now she spends her time with Jane Douglas and the Work girls. As for Lucy — but I have to stop now. I have wandered way off track, considering I started this entry with *rats*.

Later

Sarah is missing a handkerchief with the initial *S* embroidered on it. We helped her look in the school and in the dormitory but did not find it, nor did we find Maggie's blue sash. It has been gone for a week.

I have decided that if the other girls do not take to me, I may as well do as I please.

In my Future Novel I will be sure to give my Heroine a special friend, so she will not be as lonely as I am.

Thursday, August 15th

Little by little the weather is changing. The mornings are cool and foggy. The nights are chilly, so it is easier to sleep. Except for the rats.

I am discouraged and homesick. If only I were home picking berries with Nokum or gossiping with Suzanne or racing across the prairie. I felt free on the prairie, where the world stretched before me in all directions. In this place I feel as tho' the trees are caging me in.

I wish Fort Victoria were on a river instead of on the sea. The tide comes in and goes out but it does not seem to *lead* anywhere — except out to the open ocean, which must be as immense as the sky. I have heard people say that out on the ocean you can spend days and days without seeing a speck of land!

You can *follow* a river, and let the current take you wherever it pleases — to rapids or deep quiet pools, and Adventure around every bend. It leads you *onward* — and sometimes, when the current is fast-flowing, the wavelets seem to be laughing and calling out, "We're racing our way to the end!" It's all you can do to keep from racing along.

Oh, fiddle. Sarah has just come in. She wants help looking for her handkerchief and is reluctant to crawl under the beds.

Friday, August 16th

More veg. have been stolen from Rev. S's garden and he is at his wit's end. No one at school knows anything about it, tho' someone might be lying.

Rev. Staines has been asking throughout the Fort, for the thief could be a worker or a tradesman or even an officer. I am secretly pleased that a few missing lettuces can upset him so greatly.

Two weeks since I have been here, and my excitement about *Learning in a Real School* is wearing thin. Aunt Grace was strict and we had to do lessons for long periods of time, but her school was never like this.

Oh, I am so homesick!

<u>What I miss:</u>
Father
Nokum
Suzanne and her family
Fort Edmonton
Aunt Grace — for tho' she was stern and had a sharp tongue, and smacked me on occasion (and I hated her for it), she did not have a heavy hand and she did not make me sit upright on a hard bench for hours and chant *das, dat, damus* Latin
Uncle Rory

I miss the freedom I had at Fort Edmonton — being able to visit the Home Guard families and play with Nokum's great-nieces and Suzanne's cousins and help Nokum make moccasins and embroider them — oh, I miss it, I miss everyone, and now my mind is made up. Before I go to bed I'm going to write to Aunt Grace and tell her I am returning to Fort Colvile. Goodness knows when she will receive my letter, but at least it will be in the mail packet and ready to go.

There's the Supper chorus.
I wish we could eat in the Fort's dining hall for a

change and talk to the other children, but we are in class even during meals, and in the same room as well. At least Rev. Staines eats with the men, and thank goodness for that.

Friday, August 16, 1850

Fort Victoria
Dear Aunt Grace,

You were right. I do not need an Education of the sort offered here. In fact (and I do not exaggerate) I hate the school, the people, the meals, the dormitory, the Latin, the rats and Sundays. I have never felt so lonely. Last night I cried myself to sleep. (It was not the first time.)

Please forgive my Stubbornness and Pride and let me return to Fort Colvile. I will never argue or talk back or sulk and will try to behave in a more ladylike fashion.

I am sending this letter to you via the Clerk on his next visit to Fort Colvile, and I pray I will hear from you on his return.

Please give my regards to Uncle Rory.

Your loving and obedient niece,
Jenna Sinclair

I did not put my letter in the packet for Fort Colvile, I put it in my Journal to remind me of what I was going to do, before I had a change of heart. Aunt used to talk about "staying the course," even when the course appeared to be hopeless, and she'll be pleased to hear that I do have occasion to follow her advice.

The reason for my change of heart? I have a friend! We met in the most unexpected way — indeed, today was *full* of the unexpected — so I had better start at the beginning.

This morning Mrs. Staines announced that she was taking the girls on an outing to Beacon Hill "to watch the Indians harvest their camas."

She did not tell us what camas was, but I reckoned it was what I'd seen the Indians digging.

We left after Breakfast. It was great fun, everyone in a happy mood, even Mrs. Staines, and we waved gaily to the boys as we set out, for *they* were spending the morning pulling weeds in Rev. S's vegetable garden.

Lucy walked beside me until we reached the trail and then it was single file around the Bay, with Mrs. Staines leading the way and making sure no one skipped on ahead. We talked and laughed and Maggie's bonnet got caught in some sort of prickly vine because she went off the trail, and Annie found a robin's egg and Lucy screamed when she saw a hornet's nest, and the girls who were at the school last year told stories about the picnics and outings they'd had, and kept asking Mrs. Staines when we could go on a picnic this year and she said we'll make it soon while the weather is fine. (I hope she does not forget or change her mind.)

Mrs. Staines had us sit in the grass at the top of Beacon Hill, our legs tucked beneath us in a proper ladylike manner and our dresses spread out around us in "an elegant way," but my dress was not long enough. (I must have grown since Aunt Grace made it!) Mrs. S's dress sounded like a walk through autumn leaves when she sat down, the material is so crisp and crackly.

Songhees women were out digging, as I'd seen before, but in different parts of the meadow, and Mrs. Staines explained that they were digging up camas, a type of root like a potato. She said they planted potatoes too.

I saw the woman who had reminded me of Nokum. She was harvesting on the slope right below us, and whenever she began to speak, the women and children working with her fell silent, except to laugh or sigh or cry out with surprise. I reckoned she was telling stories.

Soon enough it was time to go. It took me a while to adjust my dress, and I hopped around a bit, for my legs were pins and needles from being tucked up and elegant, and so I ended up being last in line. Now I hadn't *planned* this, but when the others were well into the woods and I was still hopping about on the meadow, I saw my Lookout tree and I could not resist climbing it. Only a little ways, I decided, so I would not end up too far behind, and if Mrs. Staines scolded me for dawdling I could tell her I'd needed to go behind some bushes to relieve myself (which was in fact the truth). Anyway, Mrs. Staines was not in a scolding mood.

So up I climbed! It felt so good being away from the proper English girls and in my tree, I climbed a bit higher. Oh, the view was grand! And a bit higher still, and I recognized my perch from last week and went even higher! Well then I heard a sound that was not the rustle of branches.

I stopped and listened. A voice! "Hello," it said — from somewhere in the tree.

I was so startled I almost fell off the branch. "Where are you?" No answer but a giggle, and a rustling of branches.

The next thing I knew I was looking at a Songhees girl, standing on a branch a little lower than mine. She smiled and started to back down, indicating that I should follow.

I made to do so, but suddenly froze. Without realizing it, I had climbed a great deal higher than I had before and the ground looked impossibly far. I must have gasped or given some sort of cry, for the next thing I knew, I felt the girl's hand on my ankle, slowly guiding my foot to the next branch. Goodness, it was shaking so much it's a wonder she could hold onto it at all, but she did, speaking words of encouragement the whole time — at least that was how they sounded — and in that way I made it down, with a great number of "whews" and "thank yous" on my part.

Once we were on the ground, the girl pointed to herself and said, "Kwetlal."

"Jenna," I said, and we repeated each other's names and smiled.

As I was running to catch up to the others, I saw Lucy up ahead, coming to look for me. "We missed you," she says. "Mrs. Staines was worried."

The others were sitting on a log near the stream and, when I told them that I'd twisted my ankle and had had to limp part of the way — but it was better now — they said they'd been dawdling anyway, singing and playing guessing games, expecting I'd be along soon enough, so no harm done.

It was a glorious outing — and best of all, I might have a new friend!

Sunday, August 18th

Maggie has still not found her sash, tho' we have searched high and low. She is certain that one of us has taken it.

Some of the boys almost killed another dog from the Songhees village — like they did last week, when they caught one chasing chickens. They chased after it and when they had it cornered, they beat it to death, and boasted.

Not this time. Lucy and I were walking around the yard after Dinner and saw one of the Songhees' wool dogs by the kitchen, looking for scraps. Lucy was surprised, said she'd never seen a wool dog at the Fort, not since she'd been here, and we should try to catch it so one of the men could return it.

"We could return it ourselves!" I said.

And Lucy says, "We can't go to the village, it's forbidden!"

While we'd been talking, Alec and a group of boys had spotted the dog and were chasing it, waving sticks and throwing stones, and I cried, "Come on, Lucy!" and ran after them, yelling at them to stop, but they didn't, they chased it right through the East Gate.

By the time I caught up — Lucy hadn't gone past the gate — they had it cornered behind Father Lempfrit's cabin. "Leave it alone!" I shouted, and in true heroic fashion — I can use this in my Novel! — I grabbed Thomas's stick and pushed the boys aside. "You should be ashamed!"

They must have thought I'd turned into Mrs.

Staines! There was a lot of muttering — It's only a *dog,* We'll get the next one, etc. — and Davy threw one last stone, but then they swaggered off and left me to my rescue.

Poor little creature! He cowered when I approached, no doubt afraid of a beating, but I spoke a few comforting words and gingerly held out my hand. By and by he grew more confident, even licked my fingers and wagged his tail. Best of all, he allowed me to pet him.

It was the first time I'd seen one of the white dogs up close, or touched one, and their hair really is as thick and soft as sheep's wool. No wonder they are valued so highly!

I longed to keep him as a pet and curl up with him in the winter, but I knew I wouldn't be allowed. At least he let me pick him up and hold him — a difficult task (tho' pleasant) for he was not a puppy.

I carried him around to the escarpment, staying outside the stockade so I wouldn't stir up the Fort's dogs or run into the boys. There were some Songhees men on the beach and I called out, holding up the dog so they would see it, and set him onto the path. Off he went! Straight down to the beach and into one of the canoes. No looking back or woofing a "thank you," but I am sure he was grateful.

I told Lucy about the rescue, saying she should have stayed with me — she could have petted the dog and helped me carry it. When I asked why she had turned back, she said it wasn't proper to go chasing after boys.

Well I expect she is right — unless there is a good reason for doing so. Which is what I had.

Suzanne would have come, and we would have relived the Adventure for days afterwards. Oh, goodness, rescuing the dog has just reminded me of the time Suzanne and I found two baby rabbits. We took them into the barn where one of the cats had had kittens and the cat adopted the bunnies as if they were her own. It was the most wonderful sight — five kittens and two bunnies suckling together while the mother cat purred. Suzanne and I watched for the longest time. And when Suzanne moved a bunny away from the cat to see what would happen, the cat got up, went over to the bunny, picked it up by the scruff of its neck and took it back to the family.

Tuesday, August 20th

A mystery has been solved!

On my way back from the privy — well before Breakfast — I heard Rev. Staines saying good morning to Mr. Minie. I looked around to see where Rev. S was and spied him on the Gallery looking down at his vegetable garden. I then heard him say, "That's a fine lettuce you've got there, Minie, why not take the rest while you're at it?"

And Mr. Minie said, "Merci," and did just that.

I told the girls later, and how we laughed! Rev. Staines must have been beside himself, for the lettuce thief cannot even be punished now, since Rev. S told him to help himself!

Wednesday, August 21st

Today I went into the Trade Store. Mr. Finlayson and Mr. Durham were there. I told them I was looking for a blue sash and a handkerchief taken from the dormitory, but in truth it was to look inside the store. It was much like the one at Fort Edmonton, a treasure house of shiny brass kettles and copper pots, coloured glass beads, thick white blankets (with a black, a red and a yellow stripe), buttons, needles, clay pipes, guns, axes, knives. Copper wire, like Nokum used for making snares. The store had the same rich scent of tobacco and furs. It made me feel homesick. I failed to find the sash or the handkerchief, but was not surprised.

Friday, August 23rd

Three weeks have gone by since I arrived.

Have I learned three weeks worth of New Knowledge at Staines School? No, and Latin does not count. (*The Pains' School of Parson Puce* — that could be a title for my Novel!)

I have learned about other things though, thanks to my wanderings outside the Fort.

Saturday, August 24th

This morning I went to the meadow and saw Kwetlal again. She was digging camas with the others, tho' there were not as many as last week, which makes me think the harvest might be coming to an end. When I approached her, she remembered my name and looked happy to see me. It turns out she speaks and understands a little bit of English and when she pointed towards the Fort, mimed the act of paddling a canoe and said "brother" and "father," I guessed that she might have learned some words from a relative who works for the Company. Maybe her father or a brother was one of the paddlers who brought me from Fort Langley. We played a few more "guessing games" — including one in which I tried to explain that my mother and father were dead, but not my grandmother. I must have used the right gestures for she smiled, seeming to understand, and took me to meet *her* grandmother, the woman I had seen telling stories. I managed to get across that she reminded me of my grandmother.

I had never seen a camas root up close so I took the opportunity and looked into Kwetlal's basket. "Camas?" I said. They looked more like bulbs than roots, but Mrs. Staines had been right about the name for, on hearing "camas," Kwetlal gave a delighted grin, handed me a pointed stick and showed me how to use it. (Now I wonder if I might have pronounced "camas" incorrectly, and said something that means "Let me help with the digging.") It was not as easy as it looked.

I got better with practice, but came close to making a grave mistake. I had gone into the woods to relieve myself and, coming back, had noticed a clump of stalks that had not been touched. Thinking that the bulbs would have to be dug up eventually, I decided to be helpful by making a start. Well I'd no sooner put in the stick than Kwetlal's grandmother gave a cry of alarm and motioned for me to stop. She looked very concerned, Kwetlal too, and I soon understood why — the spot where I was about to dig was for *poison* camas. And to show how dangerous it was, she dug up a large, fine-looking bulb that looked identical to the others. *That* was why they had to be kept apart. And to make sure the one she'd dug up would not end up with the others, she reburied it then and there.

I learned a lot more — at least I *hope* I learned, for reading the language of gestures was at times as difficult as understanding Latin. Thank goodness Kwetlal knows some English. Halting it may be, but there was no mistaking her meaning when she said "Death camas." So my nature lesson on camas (or what I gathered from our conversation), is this:

There are two kinds of camas, blue and white, and the bulb from the white is poisonous. The only time you can tell them apart is when the plant is in flower, so every spring the women dig up the white plants, roots and all, and destroy them. And sometimes they move a few to a distant spot. Thank Heaven they saw where I was about to dig.

I made certain to remember where the white camas was buried, though I would never dig in the meadow without Kwetlal. It would be akin to someone digging in the Company's garden, or stealing Rev. S's vegetables.

I wish I had asked Kwetlal if they ever use the death camas on their enemies. Is that why they don't destroy all the white plants?

Oh, what a perfect idea for my Novel! The Hero could use it on a Villain, like Parson Puce or Mrs. Staines, or a Villain could use it on a group of unsuspecting girls at Staines School! Those with the most poisonous tongues, like Maggie and Sarah, would fall deathly ill, but Jenna the Heroine would be spared.

Before I left the meadow I asked Kwetlal if I could keep a camas bulb for a souvenir. She said I could, so I picked one out and hurried back to the Fort.

The girls were playing tag in the yard and asked me to join them, but I came up to the dormitory, wrapped my bulb in a handkerchief — the one with the embroidered flowers that Aunt Grace gave me —

and put it inside my deerskin pouch.

My souvenirs of Vancouver's Island now include a camas bulb, a clamshell, a blue-black mussel shell and a tiny cedar cone from my Lookout. I keep them in the pouch, next to the bag of pemmican, inside my *cassette*. I think of them as my secret treasures and do not want anyone to know.

Tuesday, August 27th

I had a disturbing dream last night. A Cree woman was trying to enter the Fort but Aunt Grace was barring her way. The woman was crying and begging to be let inside.

I cannot stop thinking of this dream. I never liked the way Aunt behaved towards the Cree. She would probably have treated my own mother in the same uppity way, had my mother been alive, and it upsets me to see Mrs. Staines behaving likewise, especially towards Mrs. Douglas. Whenever their paths cross Mrs. Staines looks down her nose in a puffed-up manner or turns the other way.

Father once told me that a year after Aunt's arrival in Fort Edmonton, she had been jilted by a man in favour of a half-breed woman, and had taken it hard, believing that a white woman should have a stronger claim on any white man. Being more uppity, I suppose.

I like Mrs. Douglas. Whenever *our* paths cross she

smiles and says hello and asks how I am doing in school. The other day she was working in her garden. I stopped to admire her flowers, and she told me that she'd brought the seeds from flowers she had grown when the family was living in Fort Vancouver. She told me their names — wallflowers, marigolds, sweet William, candytufts — I forget the rest. I thanked her in Cree, for I had heard that her mother was Cree, and she gave me the warmest smile and asked about my family, etc. So we ended up having a nice chat in Cree until the bell rang for Supper and it was time to go inside.

The Douglas girls are fortunate to have such a kind and gentle mother. I like to think that my mother would have been the same, had she lived.

Later

After Supper I joined some of the girls for a walk to Beacon Hill. Mostly the oldest girls, so Mrs. Staines gave her permission.

There was no one digging on the meadows. The mat shelters were gone, and there were piles of brush and weeds that had been dug up before. I think the camas harvest must be over.

On the way back we stopped by the stables to pet the horses. I miss the horses we had at Fort Edmonton. And the times Father would take me riding. Sometimes he would walk his horse and let me sit by myself, "to get the feel of it." I felt grand being up so high.

Thursday, August 29th

Alec and Davy got into a fight with a couple of Songhees boys. I did not see what happened, but Radish said that one boy was "punched up pretty bad." A worker at the salmon store stopped the fight and hauled our boys up to Rev. Staines. They were caned and forbidden to fight again.

Saturday, August 31st

The other night I was telling the girls about Mr. Rowand's racehorses and how thrilling it was to go to the track outside the Fort and watch the races. Sarah and a few others made a great show of yawning, and Lucy told me that everyone was bored by Fort Edmonton this and Fort Edmonton that, and they wished I would go back there or stop talking about it.

Well I flared up at this and said I would go back in an instant if I could, and maybe I *would*, so there, and stomped off in a huff.

Now I realize I was being childish, and making myself even more unlikable. I should have laughed and told them they were right — I *do* go on about Fort Edmonton — but I thought my stories were entertaining! Is that how you make a friend, by doing what *they* want? It was so easy with Suzanne. I'm glad I've met Kwetlal, even though it's a challenge understanding each other. I hope I'll see her and her grandmother again. But how, if the harvest is over?

Time for Dinner, and then Deportment.

Later

Mrs. Staines took us outside in Deportment. "Mind your step, girls! Hold up your skirts, like so! No, no, Lucy — hold them out at the sides! Like so!" She led the way on a devilish obstacle course of ruts, dips and boardwalks, dodging dogs and manure and chickens — and we followed in single file, a gaggle of giggling schoolgirls. The workers in the yard looked on with amusement and the boys who happened to be around aped our every move with outrageous exaggeration, which drove Mrs. Staines to distraction and made us giggle the harder. It was too hilarious to think of being embarrassed, although a few of the older girls looked mortified — especially when Mr. Beauchamp began to whistle and blow kisses.

Mrs. Staines said afterwards that we must learn to keep our dignity in such situations and to ignore all displays of "infantile behaviour." *Et cetera*.

We had a good laugh at the boys' expense though,

for they had to have a haircut. The wife of one of the *canadiens* does it once a month. She cuts hair as tho' she were wielding a scythe through a wheat field.

Sunday, September 1st

There was such a din in the Common Room last night, none of us could sleep, so Lucy pried up the loose board and we spied on the officers. They were having a grand time, drinking spirits and slurping oysters off the shell — raw oysters!

We tried to follow their conversation, but there was so much guffawing and slurping that they could have been speaking Latin, except that they were enjoying themselves too much.

Sarah said she had tried a raw oyster, but had not liked the feel of it sliding down her throat. That led to a discussion about the worst foods we had ever eaten. For Lucy it was roast dog and for me it was fat and gristly beaver tail — even though Suzanne and everyone else loved beaver tail and considered it a luxury.

After the men had quieted down a little and the other girls had gone to sleep, Lucy leaned closer to my bed and whispered that she wished she were more like me. I did not believe her, for she had made fun of my clothing and teased me in front of the others, but I was curious enough to ask why.

She said she wanted to be brave enough to go exploring, like I did, but was too cowardly — afraid of getting lost or hurt, afraid of Alec finding out and telling her father, afraid of being caned by Rev. Staines or captured by a hostile tribe and turned into a slave. She went through a list of such dire possibilities that I laughed and said, "Or you could be flogged on the jetty and thrown into the harbour for the crabs." Whereupon she added, "Or forced to eat boiled rat tails!"

After that we took turns adding to our list of Worst Punishments, laughing so hard we had to stop for fear of wetting our beds.

Then I told her that I knew how to poison someone.

"How?" she said, and leaned even closer, so our heads were almost touching.

"With camas." I told her all about it — how easy it would be and how no one would know the difference until it was too late.

She wanted to know how I knew, and I said it was a secret.

We were quiet after that until I heard Lucy whisper, "Can I come with you on your next adventure?" I pretended to be asleep. If she had asked me a few weeks ago I would have been pleased, and we might have become good friends. But what if she came with me and we happened to meet Kwetlal? Would Lucy take kindly to her? Would she tell Mrs. Staines that I am associating with the Songhees, something we are forbidden to do? I would rather keep my friendship with Kwetlal a secret.

Monday, September 2nd

No black treacle on our bread this morning, but *jam!* Red, syrupy, sweet, sticky, delectable! We savoured each mouthful and took such a long time doing so that Mrs. Staines said there would be *no more jam* if we were late for school.

The leaves on the maples are slowly beginning to change colour. A few have begun to fall.

The poplars along the banks of the Saskatchewan River will be bright gold by now. The mornings will be cold. Nokum might be wearing the warm *capote* of Father's I gave her — tho' the sleeves were too long and the hood almost covered her face. Soon she and the women will be hard at work mending snow-shoes in time for winter.

Tuesday, September 3rd

Another Breakfast with jam. Not a speck is wasted, for we wipe our plates clean with a finger when Mrs. Staines is not looking. I told Radish he had a bit at the corner of his mouth and he said he was saving it for later.

Another thing about today, but not as nice as

jam, is the smoke. The air has been full of it — not just today, but for the last few days — and when I asked why, Lucy told me that the Indians were burning the meadows. I did not believe her but Rev. Staines overheard us arguing and said it was true, and after Supper he is taking a group of us to see for ourselves.

Later

It is true. We walked to Beacon Hill after Supper and sure enough, some Songhees were setting fire to piles of weeds and to thick patches of fern and underbrush — even to small trees growing beneath the oaks. I was alarmed at first, fearing the fire would spread to the Fort or to my Lookout tree. But Rev. Staines said the fire would not get out of control, the Indians kept careful watch, and it is something they do every harvest. He had heard all about it from various men and officers who had been here a long time. When a few of us asked why, since it made our eyes sting and filled the air with smoke, he said he expected they had a good reason and what did we think it might be?

Lucy and I exchanged glances, thinking the same thing — Rev. Staines does not know the answer. But neither did we, so we made suggestions like the others (on our way back, for the air was too smoky to linger).

Mine: To keep bushes and shrubs from taking over their camas?

James: And their potatoes.

Alec: To make the ground easier to dig, for when they dig up the potatoes and stuff next year?

Sarah: Because it's faster to burn the weeds than to pull them out?

And more of the same, until Lucy says to Rev. Staines, "Sir, could you not just ask the Indians?"

"A splendid idea," he says.

Maybe I'll try to find out from Kwetlal. Maybe the burning is something they have been doing for hundreds of years and don't even think about why anymore. Every year the camas and other plants grow back, so the burning works, whatever the reason, and maybe that's reason enough.

Radish made us laugh when he said, "Why does every outing have to be a lesson? Can't we just go somewhere and not think?"

Wednesday, September 4th

Hot today, once the fog lifted.

Radish is missing a small wooden carving in the shape of a whale. He claimed it was taken by one of the boys. Rev. Staines ordered a search of the boys' dormitory but it was not found there, nor in ours.

<u>The missing items are now:</u>
1 blue sash
1 white handkerchief with an embroidered *S*
1 small wooden carving

Another idea for my Novel — the disappearance of various small items, or one item that is exceedingly valuable! The Fort is in a panic because the item must be found before the turn of the tide to prevent a dire catastrophe!

Back to the Staines School Mystery — who could be responsible? And why are such trifles being taken? I would love to solve the case.

Everywhere smells of salmon! The Songhees are bringing in cured and smoked salmon for trade and the salmon store is filling up.

I have heard that the most valuable fur in this district is not beaver but sea otter. Not here so much, but farther north. And I was surprised to hear that the sea otter pelts go all the way to China!

I wonder if the Chief Factors in this district are awarded 12 beaver tails as they are in the Saskatchewan District. Father loved when Mr. Rowand received his tails, for he shared with the other officers. Eugh, I can taste the gristle just *thinking* of beaver tails.

Lucy has said nothing more about accompanying me on my next Adventure. She may have forgotten, or perhaps she was not serious. I am relieved.

The wind today is driving the smoke from the camas fires right over the Fort. My nose won't stop twitching.

Thursday, September 5th

Another outing with Rev. Staines, a walk around James Bay to Laurel Point, a place where I had not yet been, and we left right after Supper — only a few of us — Sarah, Lucy, Eliza, James, Alec and Thomas. Radish called us a bunch of chowderheads, spending time with Rev. S when we didn't have to.

I thought the same, but an outing was an outing and, since the wind was blowing in a different direction, we were not bothered by smoke.

And Rev. Staines was different — pointing out plants and trees and little creatures and telling us their names (like slugs, eughh!). I was afraid he'd get so carried away with Nature Studies we would not even make it to the head of the Bay, let alone to Laurel Point. But we did!

We had a fine view from the Point, for we could look across the water at the Songhees village and down the harbour toward the Fort. There is an abundance of laurel trees — Rev. Staines said some people call them arbutus — and they shed their bark. It is a reddish-brown colour that peels off like paper, and curls! We all had to try it, and Alec stuck a few rolled-up curls behind his ears. The bare trunk is a deep orangey-gold. It feels cool and smooth to the touch.

Laurel Point is also called Deadman's Point, because it's a Songhees cemetery. There are four carved wooden figures there, as large as life, standing side by side overlooking the water, as if they are guarding the entrance to the harbour. Perhaps they mark the graves of powerful chiefs!

Rev. Staines told us we would stop there a while, as he wanted to make some jottings in his notebook. The boys were scrambling on the beach looking for crabs, the girls were watching them and I sat on a large rock jutting into the water just a little ways beyond.

I had no sooner sat down than I heard someone call my name. I spun around and saw Kwetlal and an older boy paddling a canoe. They were coming from the entrance to the harbour and were on their way home when Kwetlal spotted me and came over.

I had seen the boy before, fishing for herring, and when Kwetlal introduced us I learned that he is her brother. Try as I might, I could not pronounce his Songhees name, so he said I could call him Jimmy. He paddles for the men at the Fort sometimes, and that's what they call him. His father and uncle work as paddlers too, along with others in the village, and that is how they know a little English. As usual, our "conversation" involved gestures and guesswork, but I think I understood well enough. Jimmy's smattering of English was a big help.

By now the others had seen the canoe and were throwing curious looks in our direction — including Rev. Staines — so I joined them as Kwetlal and Jimmy paddled away.

Our walk back was faster, for the sun was going down and Rev. S was anxious to reach the Fort before dark. He even let some of us run on ahead.

And now the sun *is* down, and Mrs. Staines will be here at any moment, telling us to put out our candles. Time for one last sentence — Laurel Point is a good place to wave across to the village because Kwetlal or Jimmy might spot me and wave back. What a glorious outing!

Friday, September 6th

More jam, but from a new tin. The other has gone missing.

Alec and Davy have been trading some of their belongings. The other day I saw them on the beach with some herring fishermen and watched them trade a hat and something else for a string of dried clams and some herring. And yesterday I saw them with Mr. Beauchamp — even though Rev. Staines ordered us not to go near the smithy on account of his "filthy tongue" — and as I was walking by, I happened to see Mr. Beauchamp handing Davy a musket and some ammunition. I did not see what Mr.

Beauchamp got in return — a trifle, I expect, for the musket looked very old and rusty. But the boys looked pleased. Until they saw me.

I smiled and looked the other way.

Saturday, September 7th

I walked to Laurel Point this morning and there was Kwetlal! She was already on this side of the harbour and had seen me coming. One of her tasks is to collect herring eggs, and she does it in a clever way. Since the fish like to lay their eggs on branches, she weights cedar branches with stones, sinks them into shallow water and leaves them overnight. In the morning, she pulls up the branches and collects the eggs! I helped her wash the eggs into baskets and reset the branches, and later, in the village (yes, I went to the village!), I helped squeeze the eggs into balls to be dried.

Her village is different from the Cree camps, for there are no ponies and their shelters are not buffalo-hide tipis that can be taken down and moved when the buffalo move on, but enormous lodges made of giant cedar planks and lined with woven cedar mats. The centre of the lodge is the common area, and the rest is divided into compartments, each with its own fire. Their sleeping platforms are placed one above the other, a little like the hammocks on the *Cadboro*, but not likely to rock!

Brown dogs were sleeping or running loose throughout the village, and I did not see any of the woolly white ones. I asked Kwetlal about this through a mixture of words and actions — in this case saying "woolly white dogs," pointing to the white in my dress and howling. She found this very funny, but understood all right, and took me to the enclosure I had seen from the water the day I arrived. There was only one dog inside, not four, as I'd seen that day, and after I made a show of counting and looking puzzled, Kwetlal pointed in the direction of the strait, mimed the action of paddling, and howled in her turn. Fortunately I remembered what Mr. Douglas had said about the wool dogs being kept on a nearby island, away from the other dogs. Otherwise I might have thought that they had been taken to the mainland.

It is very frustrating to be unable to speak like we normally would, but our way seems to be working out, especially since she knows a few English words. And our game of acting out meanings is entertaining, not only for us but for anyone else who happens to be around.

I saw her grandmother again today, and met her mother and a few other relatives. The men and older boys were out fishing or hunting, or had gone up the coast to trade with other tribes. Some boys, like Jimmy, were off harpooning seals.

Kwetlal showed me a basket she was weaving,

using the soft inner bark of red and yellow cedar. She explained that it took a long time to train her fingers to weave tightly enough so that the baskets could hold water and hot stones, for they are used for cooking fish.

A lot of women were wearing HBCo blankets over their shoulders, and here's something curious — I think I saw Maggie's blue sash! A girl had it tied around her waist, but as she was on the far side of someone's lodge I did not see it clearly. If it was Maggie's, how did the girl come to have it? Not from the Trade Store, for such a sash is not a trade item. Unless one of our boys took it and used it for his own trading? Ahh! Is *this* why things are disappearing? I suspect it is! If this were my Novel I would boldly confront the ringleader — Davy, I think — and haul him off to the Chief Factor for punishment. Why, Davy is a bit like Fagin in *Oliver Twist,* who orders poor orphans like Oliver to break into houses and pick pockets.

This is only speculation — a regular Misdemeanor, it seems — and I would never accuse someone without proof. Except in a Novel.

Back to the Songhees village. The best thing about my visit to what Mrs. Staines calls "forbidden territory" was paddling the canoe. I loved the feel of the paddle and the way it cuts into the water, though it has a different feel than the lighter paddle I used in Fort Edmonton. But our canoes were lighter altogether — they were not made from the trunks of cedar trees!

Mostly everyone in the village was occupied with camas bulbs in one way or another. Some were putting red-hot stones into an enormous pit and covering them with dry grass. Others were at another pit, putting baskets of bulbs — hundreds of bulbs! — on top of the grass and covering it with branches and soil and old cedar mats. One of the women made a hole in the earth, poured in water, and plugged the hole so that the water would seep through to the bulbs and steam them. Kwetlal gave me a cooked bulb to try. It was dark brown and soft, and tasted sweet. I liked it so much I had some more.

Kwetlal said it takes a couple of days for the bulbs to cook. A long time to wait if you wanted to poison someone. If the Villain in my Novel decides to use the death camas, I will make sure he has a cooked supply on hand.

Later

Paddling back to Laurel Point might have been the best part of my visit, but the very best part was making *Soopolallie*, which you make with a bright orange-red berry that's also called *soopolallie*. Kwetlal had found enough late berries to fill a basket, and it was my good fortune to be there when she was planning to make the treat. She even let me help! We used sturdy green leaves from a bush called salal as our whipping tools, added a bit of water, and whipped the berries until they foamed into a salmon-coloured froth. It was almost too pretty to eat! Kwetlal's mother added some sugar she'd got from the Trade Store, but the *soopolallie* still tasted bitter. I didn't mind, for it felt light and frothy on my tongue. Light in my stomach, too, almost as if I'd swallowed air. *Soopolallie!* Even the name sounds light and frothy.

Sunday, September 8th

Cook is in a foul temper because yesterday another tin of jam was stolen, and it was opened but two days ago. We had treacle for Breakfast, with sour faces.

My day worsened after Breakfast, for Kwetlal had not warned me of the effects of eating camas. So all day I have been passing wind.

The ordeal began during Rev. S's sermon when Radish whispered, "Who farted?"

No mystery there, for my face must have looked as red and hot as it felt. The girls held their noses and moved as far from me as they could, and the boys did the same, covering their mouths to hold in the giggles.

Rev. Staines tried (unsuccessfully) to keep his nose from twitching. Mrs. Staines scowled and raised her handkerchief to her face, but what could I do?

After Service Mrs. Staines took me aside and asked what I had eaten to cause such misery (hers or mine?).

I told her it could have been the herrings we had for Supper, but was more likely the treacle at Breakfast. My stomach has grown used to the jam, I said, and was not happy with treacle, and was it not fortunate that no one else was afflicted?

She said, "Thank the Lord for small mercies."

I keep wondering about the Jam Thief. Is he one of us? Or one of the workers, or one of the *canadien* children, or an officer? It could be anyone. I have seen the pantry off the kitchen, and it would be easy enough to slip inside. I might have done so myself had I thought of it, or been so inclined.

Monday, September 9th

Mr. Durham came into the schoolroom (during Latin) and told us that several items have gone missing from the Company Store.

"We didn't do it," Radish blurted out.

"No one's accusing you," said Mr. Durham. He only wanted to know if any of us had been outside last night, and if we had seen anything suspicious. No one had.

Some of us asked questions so he would stay longer — we had already missed a good part of

Latin! — but Rev. Staines saw what we were up to and put an end to it by saying we must not keep Mr. Durham from his work.

There was a search throughout the Fort but nothing has been found. Who can this daring thief be? First the dormitories, then the pantry and now the Company Store! It could be Mr. Douglas's office next.

If Suzanne were here we would sneak out at night and lie in wait and catch the thief red-handed. That would be an Adventure!

The air is still a bit smoky, but not as much as before.

Tuesday, September 10th

Jam at Breakfast! Cook showed mercy and opened another tin.

Later

Another treat today!

A Company ship arrived from the Sandwich Islands after making a stop at San Francisco, and at Supper we were given an *orange*, the first I have ever tasted. It was sweet, juicy and tangy and I wanted to make it last and last and last. I put a bit of the peel inside Nokum's pouch so I can smell it and remember the taste.

Wednesday, September 11th

Sarah has just announced that the man who stole from the Company Store has been caught. The items were found in the men's barracks, stashed with the culprit's belongings. He is a *canadien* and will be punished tomorrow.

I asked her about the jam and "our" missing items but they did not turn up. Which means the other thief is still at large.

Thursday, September 12th

The thief was flogged this morning. Alec, Davy, etc. went down to the jetty to watch and told us — in gruesome detail — how the man was stripped and bound to a post and flogged with a cat-o'-nine-tails.

They were late coming into class and Rev. Staines was furious when he found out the reason. He gave them a lecture on cruelty — he, of all people — and kept them in for the rest of the day. If he becomes the Villain in my Novel I will have him stripped and flogged without mercy.

I have been trying to behave better in school. Trying not to squirm, yawn, sigh, groan, fidget, mutter, frown, scowl, argue, daydream, whisper, mutter, hum, turn around, look sideways — but it is impossible. My head turns on its own, my face shows my feelings, the hums slip out without my permission — I am like Davy that morning in church, when he said, "It wasn't me tapping, it was my fingers."

My tongue is swollen, the number of times I have bitten it to keep quiet, but I cannot control the expressions on my face. The Spy in my Novel will need more self-control than I have, to keep his thoughts and feelings — and secrets — hidden.

Friday, September 13th

I was in the yard after morning class when Lucy grabbed my arm and pulled me over to the other girls. "Tell them what you told me, Jenna," she said. "About the camas poison."

Before I could utter a word Lucy was telling them herself.

"Where did you learn that?" said Eliza.

"She learned from the Indians," said Maggie.

Then the questions began. Jenna, are you making friends with the Indians? . . . Do you like them better than us? . . . It's not very *English* of you — don't you like being English? . . . The time we went to Laurel Point, were you talking to the girl in the canoe? . . . Have you gone to their village?

"No!" I said, but they didn't believe me.

We can tell by your face, Jenna. You know you're not allowed to go to the village . . . If Mrs. Staines finds out . . . Why do you like them better than us?

and so on, and I was fumbling for an answer when the bell rang for Dinner.

I hoped that would be the end of it but, later on, Lucy took me aside and said, "You have been to the village, haven't you? You'll be caned if Rev. Staines finds out. Or Mrs. Staines."

"They won't find out," I said. "Not unless you tell them."

"I won't tell," she said. "If you do something for me in return. Remember when you promised to take me on your next adventure?"

I had *not* promised, but was not about to argue.

Well, she said she had been waiting for me to give the word, and was hurt that I had gone to the village without her. So tomorrow she wants me to take her on an Adventure. Not to the village but somewhere else.

Das, dat, damus! I told her one little fact about camas and now it's a big bother. Was I boasting about the poison? Was it pride that made me tell her?

Yes, says Aunt Grace in my mind. And she's right. I *was* proud, for I finally had the chance to tell Lucy something that wasn't about Fort Edmonton, and I thought that if she saw me as an interesting person she would like me.

It won't be such a hardship to take her tomorrow, I suppose. Though I have no idea where we will go.

What bothers me now is the way I kept saying no, as if I were ashamed of liking Kwetlal or going to the village, etc. The only reason I didn't answer truthfully was for fear of being punished. Then I would never be allowed to do anything adventurous or interesting on my own.

Until *this* happened, Maggie and Sarah and the rest have been friendlier —

I just thought of something. They must like me a little, because why else would they care where I went or what I did?

Oh here I go again, thinking and speculating too much.

The air has been free of smoke these last few days.

Saturday, September 14th

If this were a chapter in my Novel I would call it *An Eventful Day of Stolen Jam, Burnt Potatoes and Bloody Noses!*

So, to begin.

At Breakfast, Cook announced that there will be no more jam until the thief is caught and punished. No jam for Gov. Blanshard or Mr. Douglas or Mrs. Staines, or for anyone. The fourth tin has now gone missing and he is *not* opening another until the matter is solved. Because if he does, and they keep on disappearing, there will be no tins left and we will be forced to wait until the next ship arrives with provisions and that could take another year. And we boarders need not think we are being treated more harshly than the others — "'Tis true," he says, "you lot have been grumbling the loudest about unfair treatment" — because everyone has to go without, etc. etc. He did go on!

Well Lucy was ready to set out on our Adventure the moment we were excused from the table, and we left the Fort by the East Gate. At the time I did not know where we were going, only that it would *not* be to the village or to my Lookout, but we could start by going to Beacon Hill and maybe an idea would present itself. Sure enough, it did, for when we got to the hill we saw some of the boys! They were just beginning to go down to the beach, following the same trail I discovered the first week I was here. "Let's spy on the boys!" I said, and Lucy was more than eager.

We ran down the slope to the cliffs where the trail began — no danger of being seen for they were below us on the beach. When we were halfway down the trail (trying hard not to slip or giggle), we hid in a clump of bushes to see what they were up to.

There was the usual squabbling — who had to do what, etc., but it got sorted out in the usual way with Alec and Davy ordering Thomas and Radish to gather bits of wood for a fire. Once it was lit they emptied the sacks they had been carrying, and out came strings of dried clams, dried herring, some potatoes and turnips. Radish produced a half loaf of dark bread he must have gotten from the bakery.

Lucy and I grinned at each other and headed down the bank.

"Can we stay for the cookout?" I said, whereupon the boys shouted, "No!" and Alec told his sister to "go back to the nursery" and take me with her.

Lucy turned to go but I held her back. "Let's ask them about the musket they got from Mr. Beauchamp," I said loudly. "Have you shot a grouse yet, Davy? Rev. Staines loves grouse — and potatoes. Did those potatoes come from the farm? I think Mr. Douglas — "

"All right," says Davy, scowling, "but don't be a nuisance." That was an end to it, for Davy is the "chief factor" of that little group.

We feasted on clams and herrings while the potatoes and turnips were roasting in the fire, licked our fingers, talked, teased, laughed — it reminded me of my journey with the Fort Colvile brigade, but without the mosquitoes. For a few moments I felt utterly content. It was like being with friends!

Radish was the first to notice the canoe. "The savages are attacking!" he cried, and ran down to the shore, stick in hand, to warn them off.

I went after him and told him to stop being stupid. Then I looked out at the canoe and recognized Jimmy. I waved and called out, "Hello, Jimmy!" I thought they would continue on their way, but they paddled into the cove, beached their canoe and got out, Jimmy and two other boys.

"I know you." Alec pointed at Jimmy and laughed in a nasty way. "I gave you a good whipping. Remember?"

Things happened so quickly after that I hardly know who started the fight. There was a lot of name-calling, a shove and a push, then more shoves, harder, and before I knew it, Alec and Davy and Jimmy were throwing punches and the others were doing the same and Lucy and Radish were whooping and dancing around, egging them on, and I was screaming at them to stop. Then Jimmy had Alec pinned to the ground and Alec was bleeding from his nose and his mouth and the others went quiet and Jimmy kept saying, "Who's beat now?!" and at last Alec gave up and gasped, "I am! I'm beat."

But once he was back on his feet and the boys were paddling away, he yelled, "I'll get you next time, you — "

What followed were words I cannot bring myself to write.

And then of all things, Lucy said it was *my* fault! She said the boys would not have come onto the beach if I hadn't invited them, and she accused me of *encouraging* Jimmy to beat up her brother.

She was right about it being my fault, for if I had not called out or waved they would have continued on their way and nothing would have happened. I suppose it was an invitation of sorts, tho' not intended.

The boys returned to the Fort long after Lucy and me. They might have been hoping that their bruises would disappear before they ran into Rev. Staines but, as Fate would have it, Rev. Staines was at the carpenter's shop, talking to Mr. Yates, and he saw them coming through the gate. They were all caned, twice as many strokes as the last time, because they had already been warned against fighting.

Sunday, September 15th

Something dreadful has happened to Alec. He woke everyone in the night — the dormitory walls are such that *everything* can be heard — and he was vomiting, crying, screaming with stomach pain. Such a commotion, with people going up and down the stairs — Rev. Staines, Mrs. Staines, Dr. Benson — and now it is time for Sunday Service and Alec is no better. He swears he is dying, that the Indians tried to kill

There's the bell — must go.

Later

The day has taken an unexpected turn, and I am miserable beyond despair.

Dr. Benson came to our dining room at Dinner. He told us that Alec is violently ill and delirious, and has been vomiting, purging and suffering from acute pain for *hours* — and did we know if he had had anything unusual to eat or drink?

"He had uncooked potatoes from the cookout," I said.

"But everyone ate the same and nobody else got sick," says Davy.

"Except Alec ate *more* than anybody else," says Radish.

Then Lucy jumps in. "He took ill so sudden, he must have been poisoned. That's what he told me."

"Poisoned?" says Dr. Benson. "How so?"

"Jenna poisoned him with her camas."

"What?!" I was so taken aback I almost laughed. The notion was ridiculous! "Why would I do that?"

"Because of the fight." Turning back to Dr. Benson she says, "Jenna was mad at Alec because he started the fight with her Indian friends and so she poisoned him, because she knows all about the death camas, and how to use it. And she even has some death camas. I saw her put it in her *cassette*."

Her words filled me with dread. The bulb I had kept as a souvenir — was it from a blue camas? Could I have kept a white one by mistake? I could not remember!

Dr. Benson was saying, "Now Lucy, you're upset about your brother, do you not think your imagination . . ."

Mrs. Staines was saying it was a serious matter to accuse someone of poisoning.

Sarah was telling Dr. Benson how I had bragged about having the poison.

And then Dr. Benson was telling us not to worry, we would get to the bottom of it, and he left to see to Alec, and Mrs. Staines said it was time for the Collects, and I have never been as fervent in reading prayers, especially the Collect for Aid against all Perils — tho' of course there was no mention of a peril called Lucy.

After Collects I opened my *cassette* and took out my pouch — my intention being to show Dr. Benson that I could not have used a camas bulb to poison Alec because there it was, and to prove it was harmless I would eat it in front of him — but I opened the pouch only to find that the bulb was gone, along with the knotted handkerchief I had wrapped around it.

And the handkerchief was white. It had flowers embroidered on it, but all the same — Oh, no, did I use white to remind me of the type of bulb? I *cannot* remember!

Monday, September 16th

All last night I lay awake in despair. What type of bulb had I kept? Who stole it and why? How long has it been missing?

All day I felt guilty, tho' I have done nothing wrong.

How could Lucy accuse me of something so wicked?

I admit I have *thought* of poisoning someone, but only in a Novel, and the victim would be a Villain who deserved such a fate. Alec is a scrapper but he is not a Villain.

Lucy spent most of the day in the sick room with Alec, and ignored me the rest of the time.

Oh, *mon dieu*, what will become of me if Alec dies?

I never imagined that coming to school would result in my being on trial for murder. Will they hang me? Radish says probably not, because I am a girl and not very old. He said it to cheer me up.

How will I tell Aunt Grace?

Tuesday, September 17th

Alec is better and two mysteries have been solved.

The cause of his illness was not from eating poison, but from eating too much jam taken from a tin that had been "doctored" to catch the thief. And the thief is Alec!

Mr. Field and Cook came up with the idea and carried out the plan — which was to add a grain or two of tartar emetic to a newly-opened tin of jam, and wait for someone to show the symptoms. They had not reckoned on the thief eating the *whole* tin — little wonder Alec was so ill.

Dr. Benson was horrified. He explained that tartar emetic, though useful in treating certain diseases, has "toxic side effects" and is *poisonous* if used in high amounts.

They should have let us in on their secret sooner and I told them so.

They agreed, and apologized to me and the others. Their reason was to make the culprit suffer from anxiety and discomfort.

I wish I could have been in the sick room last night. According to Mr. Field, he and Cook paid Alec a visit and asked how he was and what he had eaten, and Cook looks up and says, "Mr. Field, what became of the jam that I poisoned for the rats?" Whereupon Alec cried out, "Rat poison? I ate that jam! I'm dying!" And then he had another fit of vomiting.

No one feels sorry for him, not even Lucy, and his friends are put out because he never shared the good jam. We were certain Rev. Staines would give him a whipping, ill or not, but he said that the tartar emetic was "fitting punishment for the crime."

The punishment that Lucy caused me to suffer was not fitting, not when I had committed no crime. And I am still suffering. My stomach is a huge knot of misery. To think that Lucy could take something I told her in secret and throw it back in such a twisted and hateful way — well now she is on my list of Villains and Traitors.

She should apologize too, for saying what she did, and she should have to do so in front of everybody, and be made to suffer for betraying me.

Wednesday, September 18th

<u>Items missing from the dormitories:</u>
1 white handkerchief with an embroidered *S*
1 blue sash
1 small wooden carving
1 camas bulb tied up in a handkerchief embroidered with flowers

I wish Aunt Grace and Uncle Rory were here so I could tell them about the jam thief — right away, before the story loses its freshness. How they would laugh! I can just hear Uncle Rory and his roaring har-har-hars! The sound alone could make me laugh, even if I hadn't heard what was funny. It had the same affect on Aunt — I remember how we would look at each other and giggle, and the giggle would become a full-blown laugh and before long we'd be holding our stomachs and wiping away tears — and Uncle Rory would say, "Heck, it wasn't that funny! Har-har-har," and that would set us off again.

Well, no wonder Aunt Grace was smitten. And maybe that's why she changed after she was married — all that laughing and good humour, there wasn't time to be cross or count Misdemeanors —

Fiddle, I'm thinking too much again. At least it's taken my mind off that traitorous Lucy.

Thursday, September 19th

Stormy and cold like yesterday.

I asked Mr. Durham if some of us could look in the fur loft for our missing items. He took us there after Dinner but we did not find anything. The truth is I only wanted an excuse to see the loft.

It was empty though, as the furs that were here have been loaded onto the *Norman Morison.*

I told Mr. Durham that Father would sometimes let me help in the loft over the winter, when he and the Clerk were weighing and packing the furs. I wanted to say more but Sarah and Eliza were rolling their eyes with impatience.

I'm a little sad now, thinking of Father. He'd quiz me on weights, measures, sums and the like — once I teased him by saying he'd forgotten I was a girl and was training me to be a Company Clerk. He assured me he was doing nothing of the sort, and said I was growing into a fine young lady, thanks to Aunt Grace's lessons, and would one day be worthy of sitting at the Governor's table. "I don't want to!" I remember saying. "I only want to sit at yours."

Friday, September 20th

Alec has fully recovered, and persists in talking about his "near-death" ordeal, with gut-twisting detail.

Lucy has still not apologized, the coward. I heard that she was so anxious about Alec she lost her senses and was ready to fix the blame on anyone or anything, but that is no excuse. She did not only accuse me, she made me think I really might have been guilty — not of using the poison, but of having it available —

Oh, now *I'm* losing my senses. I have to stop dwelling on this but I can't! Which camas bulb did I keep?

Saturday, September 21st

Well I am a *tête de mouton* and that's a fact. What was I thinking? Of course I did not have a poisonous bulb — I never even dug one up! It came to me this morning on my way back from the privy, how Kwetlal's grandmother had stopped me the moment she saw where I was digging. And after she'd dug it up to show how similar the bulbs are, she reburied it most carefully. So my thoughts have tormented me for nothing. No, not for nothing, because I can use it in a Novel! With traitorous Lucy as the Villain.

Sunday, September 22nd

All week the weather has been cold and damp, except in the afternoons when the fog lifts and the sun manages to break through. How I miss the wide blue skies over Fort Edmonton, and the brittle clear bite of the prairie cold. The grey skies that hang above this place are a suffocation.

I mentioned as much after Collects and the Douglas girls laughed and said, "Wait until November."

A Royal Navy ship sailed into Esquimalt today.

Monday, September 23rd

The *Norman Morison* left today for London. She was supposed to leave eight days ago but the weather was too stormy. (I have learned that we are supposed to call a ship "she," not "it.") Rev. Staines took us to the jetty to see her off and taught Latin at the same time. *A Mari usque ad Mare.* From sea to sea.

We waved and hollered *bon voyage,* the sailors and passengers waved back, the men on the Gallery fired the cannon, and flags and pennants flew from the masts and rigging — a thrilling sight! They will be at sea for five months or more, sailing from the Pacific Ocean to the Atlantic by going south and around Cape Horn, then north to England! In another year the ship will be back with new supplies and provisions (and fashionable dresses for some, I suppose), and new workers for the Company and new settlers for the Colony.

Davy says he is praying that the next time the ship leaves, Rev. Staines will be on board.

We took as long as we could going back to the schoolroom, stopping to pick up a shell on the beach or to catch our breath climbing up the embankment or to visit the privy — until Rev. Staines started shouting. Once inside he had us label the continents and oceans on a map of the world and mark the ship's voyage. It was an unexpectedly *enjoyable* lesson, especially when he described his voyage to Vancouver's Island with Mrs. Staines and Horace. He even let Horace talk about rounding Cape Horn and the terrifying storms and the *mal de mer* and so on. He then asked if we had any questions! *Quelle surprise!*

We were hoping the questions would last until Dinner but, after only fifteen minutes, Rev. Staines remembered that he was a Latin teacher and went back to *damus ignoramus et cetera.*

A voyage on the Home Ship would be a good addition to my Novel, but I would first have to take the voyage myself to know what it is like.

Saturday, September 28th

A trip to the village with Kwetlal!

Her mother and grandmother were working with

dog wool, and I watched for a while, thinking how much it would interest Nokum, the way they mix the wool from the dogs with the long hair from mountain goats, to make the yarn strong. At least I'm fairly certain Kwetlal meant "mountain goat," for I remember seeing them on our journey through the Rockies. Their hair was shaggy and warm-looking and very long — perfect for weaving into blankets. The Songhees must get the goat wool by trading with people from the mainland.

Kwetlal's grandmother let me touch the partly-finished blanket on her loom, and it felt exceedingly soft. I cannot imagine why anyone would want a blanket from the Trade Store, though in fairness, the Company blankets are also soft and warm. Perhaps it is the novelty of having something different. It must also take a very long time to make a Songhees blanket.

Later

Lucy apologized at Supper in front of everyone. She said she was so afraid that Alec was dying, she lost her senses and was ready to blame anyone, and she'd only thought of the camas because Alec was certain he'd been poisoned. She said she hoped we could be friends.

I said we could, but I don't know. A friend is someone you can trust, like Suzanne. She never told tales about me, not even the time we were pretending we were on a brigade, and I took one of Father's pipes and a pinch of his tobacco and we snuck inside Rev. Rundle's chapel to smoke it. *Tried* to smoke, for it only made us cough and feel sick. Goodness, if Aunt Grace had found out I would still be wearing the scars.

One of the coast ships arrived from Fort Langley and the men are unloading casks of salted salmon by the hundreds. The casks stay here until the ship comes in from the Sandwich Islands, then they get loaded onto *that* ship and off it goes. Mr. Durham told me. And shingles, too, that the Songhees cut from cedar. I hope the ship comes in with more oranges.

Monday, September 30th

The Royal Navy ship left for Fort Rupert this morning, with cannon fire, etc. Governor Blanshard was on board. At Dinner Alec announced that the Governor was going in order to investigate the deaths of the British seamen — the ones he told us about before. He said that those responsible would likely be sent to the gallows, and the reason a Royal Navy ship was going instead of a Company ship was because the Marines (the men in the Navy) are armed and trained to do battle, in case there is any trouble.

Lucy looked homesick yesterday when the ship left for Fort Rupert.

I must be homesick too, for all I can think of is Fort Edmonton. This is the time of year that the brigades would come home from Hudson's Bay, sometimes early, like last year, sometimes late, but always in September or October, before the rivers froze up. I used to picture Father among the men, as they loaded the goods from the Home Ship onto the big York boats and set off across the country. Six months they'd be away, from the time they left — small wonder their return was a time of celebration and festivities! And after their arrival the Cree would come to the Fort, and all the Plains tribes — wanting to trade in their Made-Beaver tokens for new supplies. It was an exciting time, and it went on for days and days, with so many comings and goings. The year that Aunt Grace came to Fort Edmonton, there were 500 tipis outside the stockade!

There were *always* comings and goings at Fort Edmonton. People would stop there a while, before going down the Saskatchewan to the East, or making the portage to Fort Assiniboine — like I did! — on their way to the West. (Just writing those names is making me homesick.) There is no passing *through* Fort Victoria, not in the same way. It marks the beginning of a journey or the end of one.

Comings and goings. That was Fort Edmonton. Whatever made me think that my life there was dull? I suppose it was because I did not always want to stay behind and wait for the brigades. I wanted to go with them and have my own Adventures. I never realized that leaving a place would also mean leaving something behind.

Wednesday, October 2nd

I think *Lucy* must have taken my camas. She said she had seen me put it in my *cassette,* but she could not have done so, for when I came back from the meadow that day, she was outside playing tag with the other girls. And *she* was the one who asked me to join them. So I was alone in the dormitory. And the night I told her about the death camas, I never said I *had* any, so how did she know? By snooping inside my *cassette,* that's how.

Did she take it? Has she been pilfering from the others as well? How do I approach her with such a question when I have no proof?

I can't, that's all. It would be doing the same thing to her as she did to me.

Thursday, October 3rd

I have just come back from my Lookout. I did not see anyone except for Alec and Davy etc. hunting grouse. They were armed with their "new" musket, the one I saw them getting from Mr. Beauchamp, and I was afraid they might fire it the way they throw stones — with reckless abandon! I dared not twitch for fear they might mistake me for a grouse or a squirrel or something else worth shooting — a *girl* would be enough for Thomas.

I suppose I need not have worried, as they have never succeeded in hitting a grouse, or any of the other game birds that abound in the meadows and oak groves. Lucky for us that the men are better stalkers, because fresh grouse — and once some pheasant — has been a welcome change from salmon or mutton.

My biggest fear was that the boys would spot me and discover my Lookout. Fortunately they did not stay around long enough to discover anything.

I must have a Spy in my Novel. He will discover things and keep them secret until they are needed — as proof of a crime, for instance, or as an act of revenge. Or unless he is captured and forced to reveal them. The Spy could be a Hero or a Villain, I haven't decided.

List of Spy possibilities:
Radish — small, quick on his feet, tells lies with an air of innocence (at least to Rev. Staines) and he already has a "code name" (tho' it is not serious enough for a Spy)

Lucy — she is an experienced snoop
Jenna — she has already discovered a Spy Hole

Friday, October 4th

Rev. Staines is taking the boys on an all-day expedition tomorrow, up the Arm and through the Gorge. He has hired a large canoe and a full crew from the village.

I asked if the girls could join them.

No, he said, the girls would not have the necessary stamina or courage, and when I assured him that I would, his answer was the same. So I pointed out that *no one,* not even the boys, would need stamina if the Indians were doing all the paddling. Where-upon he called me "an insufferable and bothersome young lady" who ought to know better than to question her elders.

Damus Ignoramus Disappointus.

Doesn't Parson Puce know that I have travelled by horse and boat and canoe, and crossed the Athabasca Mountains on foot (except for a bit on horseback, at the beginning), and I have camped out for days and weeks on end? And that I have galloped over the prairie in pursuit of buffalo? (Well, that is not exact-ly true, not in the way I would have liked it, for I was with Father on his horse, and the buffalo were specks in the distance, but I imagined we were chasing them, and sometimes I would take aim with my imaginary bow and arrow.) It bothers me to be treated as a fragile lady creature, and that the other girls are contented to be so. If Suzanne were here, she would help convince Parson Puce of our worthiness in matters of stamina.

I had not expected that school would force me to become a different sort of person. Even Aunt Grace allowed me to be myself outside of lessons — tho' she did not always like it. And in her classes, of course we had to behave like proper young ladies.

Saturday, October 5th

Went to Laurel Point after Breakfast and was watching some land otters playing near the rocks when who should I see but Kwetlal and Jimmy paddling towards me. I told them about the boys' outing to the Gorge by pointing in that direction, and Jimmy indicated that we could do the same. (He had a bruise under one eye but he did not mention the fight on the beach and nor did I.)

I sat low in the canoe and turned my head as we passed the Fort, but caught a glimpse of Rev. Staines and the boys on the jetty, waiting for their canoe. We had a good head start.

It was a fine sunny morning, with a nip in the air and the water as still as a looking glass. Perfect for paddling and, since there was an extra paddle in the canoe, I was able to practise. It wasn't long before I was used to the weight of the paddle and could manage without creating too much of a splash. (Although the splashing was fun!)

The Gorge is narrow, with steep rocks on either side. We paddled through without difficulty, as the tide had not yet turned, and continued to the head of the Arm. Save for the two fallen logs that serve as a footbridge across the Gorge, there was no sign of habitation or people, and no sounds but bird calls and the drips from our paddles. We floated lazily for a while, spotting herons, bald eagles, numerous ducks and several deer.

We had almost reached the Gorge on the return trip when we heard singing. The boys were coming! We quickly turned to shore, and stayed hidden in the thick underbrush until they were out of sight.

By then the tide was running swiftly and the Gorge was turbulent with rapids. Jimmy

Time for Dinner.

Saturday afternoon

My blisters betrayed me and I am Confined.

Why can they not send me to the Bastion? It would be much more Adventurous than being sent "to bed." I must find out if there are any prisoners at the moment, and if I might visit them. My Novel must have a prisoner. A wrongfully accused prisoner would be best, because I know how he would feel.

Tho' I am yet again a prisoner (of sorts), I have not been punished unfairly and have no one to blame but myself. How was I to know that Mrs. Staines would be teaching "raising one's hand to be kissed by a gentleman" and would notice my blisters?

"What have we here?" she said, in her imperious manner. She was playing the role of a gentleman and had taken hold of my hand, causing me to wince with pain. Thinking something was amiss, she turned over my hand and discovered the swollen red sores, some broken and bleeding, at the base of each finger.

"These must be painful," she said. "What might have caused them?"

I was trying to think of a reasonable excuse — hoeing the garden, shovelling manure, hammering nails — when Annie said that she'd gotten blisters like that from paddling a canoe and her mother had treated them with some kind of smelly ointment to take the pain away and maybe Mrs. Staines had some. Dear little Annie, she was only trying to be helpful.

Of course Mrs. Staines asked if I had been paddling a canoe and if I had gone up the Arm like the boys.

I told her the truth, except for mentioning Kwetlal or Jimmy, and here I am.

So, to continue my account.

Jimmy asked if I wanted to go ashore and make a portage, but I said I wanted to shoot the rapids. Oh, what an Adventure! I did not even mind the soaking — in fact I wanted to do it again!

A short time later we heard the boys coming back. We watched in secret, to see how they would manage the rapids, but Rev. S made them go ashore, fortunately on the opposite side from us, and their paddlers did it alone.

It was thrilling to watch *them* go through the Gorge. On their first attempt they were caught in a whirlpool, spun around and around and thrown back out, still above the footbridge! They tried again, with a great deal of whooping, and succeeded.

The boys were watching from the bridge, but afterwards they headed into the forest. I now know that they were following a well-trodden trail, and that Rev. Staines was giving them a lesson in Natural History. James said later that Rev. Staines is a different person when he is rambling in the woods, and it's true — the evening we took the Nature Walk to Laurel Point he was *interesting*! He pointed out plants and insects — whatever caught his attention — and made notes and sketches, and encouraged us to be observant and to ask questions. All the more reason that girls should have been allowed to go on the outing, for we enjoy a ramble in the woods, and is Natural History not a worthy subject?

We made good speed on our return, eager to out-run the boys — oh, dim-witted me, I just remem-bered. There was no need to rush back (except for Dinner) for the boys are gone for the whole day.

An Unexpected Discovery!

I had finished my assigned schoolwork and was nodding off from boredom when I heard a commo-tion down below. Not down below in the Common Room, but in the empty room beneath my secret Spy Hole!

In an instant I had pulled back Annie's rug, removed the knot from the hole, and knelt down to spy. A newcomer was moving in! A Kanaka carrying a trunk came into view, followed by Mr. Durham and another man, each carrying a *cassette* and what-not, and everything was set down and they were talking about Fort This and Fort That and at one point I heard Mr. Durham say, "Well, Cavendish?" So now I know the new man's name!

It was exceedingly difficult to stay still. I dared not stir as much as a finger, or sniff or clear my throat — thank Heaven I did not sneeze! And if I happened to lose sight of them — for they kept moving about — I could not squirm into a better position.

I listened hard though, and learned a great deal about Mr. Cavendish — how he had arrived in

Hudson's Bay on the Home Ship in July ("wretched-ly sick" the whole way), then travelled with the west-bound brigade from York Factory to Fort Edmonton, then with a small party carrying leather goods to Fort Langley and finally, by canoe, to Fort Victoria. I also heard that he is to be the new Clerk.

I was relieved when they went out, for I was anxious to stretch, and write everything down. At last, someone to spy on! And not an ordinary-looking Clerk, but a handsome, dashing one — if the little I saw is any indication. He has an English accent, but does not sound uppity-stuffy like Rev. Staines, and I did not hear him mention Cambridge or Latin or anything dull like that.

I cannot wait until the girls come in so I can tell — but no, I will not be able to say a word.

Not without revealing my Spy Hole.

Sunday, October 6th

At bedtime last night there was no end of talk about the new Clerk. It was Mr. Cavendish this, Mr. Cavendish that. The other girls have already decided he is a good prospect for a husband. As for me, he will be a *perfect* Hero in my Novel!

It was a struggle for me to keep quiet, but I oohed and aahed with the others as they discussed his dark wavy hair, his deep brown eyes and the fetching dimple in his chin.

He was at Service, of course, and we were hoping he might turn his attention on us as we were filing out of the Hall — we had led the hymn singing so he *had* to have noticed us — but he was conversing with other officers and did not even glance our way. I cannot wait until next Sunday!

Monday, October 7th

I have another reason for liking Mr. Cavendish. Besides being friendly and handsome, and having the good sense to move into the room below my Spy Hole, he brought a packet of letters from Fort Edmonton, and one of the letters was for me!

He came to us at Breakfast and asked Mrs. Staines for Jenna Sinclair, and handed me the letter in person, saying, "It takes long enough for a letter to arrive, not to deliver it at the earliest opportunity."

I thanked him and he smiled — and for a few moments I was the envy of the other girls.

My letter is from Suzanne. I am eager to read it — my first thought was to tear it open right then and there, but a second thought held me back. There could be bad news in the letter. For even though Suzanne promised to write, and I desperately hoped that she would, I never truly believed she would. Unless there was a very important reason, and possibly not a happy one. And I would not want to discover it with the others looking on.

Tuesday, October 8th

5 juli

deer frend Jenna I hurt to say you that your grandmamma is died the 3 julli at the river they find her. and Evrybody love her. and my hart is ake for you.

Suzanne

I put Suzanne's letter in my Journal so I do not have to write the words.

Thursday, October 10th

I haven't had the heart to write until now, and still it is hard. When I opened Suzanne's letter I feared the worst, knowing that *one* day I would hear that Nokum was gone — but the news still caught me off guard. It is so *final*. To think that I will never see her again . . .

On Monday, after Dinner, I took the letter to my Lookout so I could read it without being disturbed.

I cried and cried, the way I did when Father died, and I wanted to stay in the tree and never go back to School or see anyone again.

Now it is evening. I came to bed without Supper

and ate a bit of pemmican. Then I lay on my bed, clutching Nokum's deerskin pouch and sobbing into my pillow.

Suzanne did not say how Nokum died. I like to imagine her walking by the river, for one "last time," and ending up on the prairie grass without even knowing she'd fallen.

Friday, October 11th

I have trouble understanding that Nokum has died. All this time I have been thinking about her as though she were still alive, yet she has been gone from the prairie for over three months.

I was surprised that Suzanne wrote in English, knowing how she hated it and how she must have struggled. And she did it on her own. Perhaps it is her way of showing how much she cared — a special effort she could make for me, since we are so far apart.

Later

I had two thoughts today. Nokum has died, and I cannot go back to Fort Edmonton.

Then it came to me that if I were there, I might feel the loss even more keenly than I do now, because everything I did or saw or heard would remind me of her. Or would that be a comfort?

Oh, I cannot write about this any longer.

We had the best Deportment Class yesterday, and my stomach still aches from laughing. It felt good to come out of my sadness.

The weather was mild, so Mrs. Staines decided to "walk us" around the yard, stressing the importance of doing so gracefully. Her outdoor lessons always attract attention, for we walk in her wake in single file, like ducklings, while she waddles (*gracefully*) at the head of the line.

The boys were playing cricket in the yard and a few of the men had joined them, including Mr. Cavendish. Try as she might, Mrs. Staines could not keep us from turning our heads — most of us showing an interest in cricket we had never shown before! The older girls ahead of me went so far as to whisper behind their hands and flutter their eyelashes. "What flirts!" Lucy said.

"Hold your skirts well out to the sides!" said Mrs. Staines, looking over her shoulder. "Eyes downcast! Do not turn your heads! *Attention, Mademoiselles!* No brazen stares!"

We did as she instructed, but a moment later our eyes went back to Mr. Cavendish. Whereupon he removed his hat and made the sweeping bow of a cavalier, playing so much the *gallant* that Mrs. Staines stumbled, let go her skirts and flung out her arms to keep her balance! If Mr. Cavendish had not caught her she would have fallen face first into the dirt! *Everyone* found this hilarious — in truth, I have been hoping for some time that such a fall would "befall" her — but we managed to cluster around and look concerned until she had composed herself sufficiently. Only when we were back in line did we start to giggle, and we have been giggling ever since — even this morning, as we were "following our leader" to Sunday Service.

I was thinking of Nokum during the Service and suddenly felt her presence so strongly it was as if she were sitting beside me — like that time I was in the Lookout — and she was bringing me comfort and telling me I need not feel sad or alone.

Wednesday, October 16th

School has been better of late because Rev. Staines has been absent. A day here, two days there, *three* days last week — and it has been this way since the beginning of October. Everyone is in a happier mood when he is not flailing his switch and growling.

Something else made us happy today — apples! One of the coast ships arrived from Fort Vancouver with a bushel of apples sent to Mrs. Douglas. We were given one each at Supper.

Someone had taken apple seeds from England to Fort Vancouver and planted them there. After Supper Lucy and I planted our apple seeds at the edge of the farm.

Thursday, October 17th

A bitter cold morning — and a shock, when the past few days have been so fine. I was shivering long before the morning bell, and hastened to put on the *capote* that my mother had made. She must have trapped animals and traded their pelts to get the blanket to make it, and fashioned it after the ones the *canadiens* wear. I love the way she decorated the long fringes with beads, and the way they swing. Father told me that she was wearing the *capote* the day he decided to make her his wife. (Though I do not think he married her because of the coat!) He kept it after she died, knowing I would grow into it and might like to wear it.

I belted it with my *ceinture fléchée* and went off to Breakfast with even more fringes swinging. The others teased me a little, but I didn't mind, for the teasing was good-natured and open, not snickers behind my back. And after Breakfast when Radish said, *"Vive la canadienne,"* I could not resist, but started singing the paddling song I'd learned from Suzanne's family, and those who knew it joined in.

Well that warmed me up, for I was paddling my imaginary canoe to mark the time — which kept getting faster — and so we paddled back and forth across the room from the meal side to the school side until Mrs. Staines came in and told us to stop.

I had also put on knitted stockings and flannel undergarments because of the cold, but what a mistake! It was not long before I began to perspire, and by the time I was able to change my clothing, I was exceedingly itchy and uncomfortable. The cold here is not like the cold in Fort Edmonton — a lesson I must learn before winter. Unless we have a *proper* winter here with snow and below-freezing temperatures. Even Fort Colvile had a proper winter.

Sunday, October 20th

Lucy was crying last night. I asked what was wrong, and she told me she missed her mother and wanted to go home and see her before she died.

"Is your mother ill?" I whispered.

"No," she says, still sobbing, "but your grandmother died before you could see her again and it made me think of my mother . . . "

Before long we were both crying — Lucy for her mother and me for mine, and for Father and Nokum — and when we were worn out with tears we hugged each other and went back to sleep.

I never thought that Lucy might be missing her mother the way I miss my family. I never gave a thought to how *anybody* else might be feeling, I only thought of how they were making *me* feel. Aunt

Grace was right, Self-Absorption is a serious Misdemeanor. I must try to overcome it.

Monday, October 21st

Another splendid day without Latin. Thomas asked if Rev. Staines was ill — a little too hopefully — but Mrs. Staines assured us that he is in good health.

Thomas groaned with disappointment. Actually, the reason for the parson's absence hardly matters, as long as he remains absent. I like to think he has been captured and enslaved. Lucy swears he stowed away on the *Norman Morison* — until we reminded her that he was with us when the ship sailed off *a mari usque et cetera*.

Wednesday, October 23rd

We now know the reason for Rev. S's absence. He has bought land in Metchosin (a few miles west of here, beyond Esquimalt) and he is going to establish a farm. A *pig* farm!

Mrs. Staines told us we can expect more absences in the future. Hurray! We could not help but cheer out loud.

Friday, October 25th

More fun in the dormitory, for now Lucy and I not only play the part of Mrs. Staines, *la grande dame,* but also that of Parson Puce, *fermier de cochons.* Then we started making up Latin-sounding words for pig. Our best one is *porcus stinkiforus gruntus.*

Raising pigs is the last thing we would have expected of Rev. S, tho' as Lucy pointed out, there is a certain resemblance.

Sunday, October 27th

We have had few quiet nights since the arrival of Mr. Cavendish. The officers gather in the Common Room and smoke and talk until all hours — sometimes quietly but more often not.

Last night they were particularly boisterous and, as I could not sleep, I decided to get up and go to the privy, thinking the cold air and exercise might make me tired. On my way back I saw a ghostly apparition in the corridor — thin, gaunt, clothed in night attire, completely white, with long hair tied in an untidy braid, and bearing a lighted candle. I flattened myself against the wall in the hopes that it would not notice me, and when it glided by I almost cried out in shock, not from fear but from astonishment, for it was Mrs. Staines!

A moment later I heard her pounding on the door of the Common Room. "Stop your racket!" she shouted. "Don't you know there are young scholars trying to sleep?"

The officers quieted down after her outburst and we were able to sleep.

Wednesday, October 30th

It has been weeks since anything has gone missing, but now Annie's locket is gone. It's a pretty one, made of silver, and she is heartbroken. We looked through the dormitory, etc. but to no avail.

Tuesday, November 5th

Today is Guy Fawkes' Day and Mr. Cavendish wanted to have a bonfire in the yard and burn the effigy of the notorious traitor. While we were rummaging for old clothes and straw to "make" Guy Fawkes, Lucy taught me a verse. We never celebrated Guy Fawkes' Day at Fort Edmonton, not that I can remember, but as it happened it was raining too hard for a bonfire. Sarah said we could save our effigy and use it as a scarecrow in the garden.

Here is Lucy's verse:

Remember, remember the fifth of November,
Gunpowder, treason, and plot.

I know of no reason why gunpowder treason
Should ever be forgot.
Guy Fawkes, Guy Fawkes

I forget the rest.

Thursday, November 21st

Since the beginning of November the days have been endlessly dreary and so much the same I stopped writing in my Journal — until now, and only for something to do. I have no Adventures to record, no Spying to report, no Visitors to describe, no new items gone missing and no missing items found.

Each day brings a monotony of rain or the threat of rain. Dark grey skies. A heaviness in the clouds that presses down on our little world, making everyone gloomy and short-tempered. Even Mr. Cavendish looks gloomy.

What makes it even more unbearable is the fact that, according to those who are used to the west coast, this weather is *normal* and will likely go on until *March!*

The Fort is knee-deep in mud and the boys have taken to sliding down the embankment, using a board as a sled.

Everything is a monotony. School, meals, Sundays — the only thing different is that Mrs. Staines is more demanding with regard to our cleanliness, now that there is an abundance of water with which to wash and bathe.

Rev. Staines is here more often because of the rain. But when he is not, I amuse myself by picturing him slopping about in the mud with his pigs. Does he practise his sermons on the poor creatures? Or speak to them in Latin? No, I think he only grunts.

Saturday, November 23rd

A few of us were jumping on Sarah's bed for something to do — much to the delight of the younger girls — when Mrs. Staines burst in without warning. "What is the meaning of this?" she shouted. "You are worse than savages" . . . "You are setting a bad example" . . . "You are a disgrace," etc., and added that since we were *behaving* like savages we could sleep on the bare floor — whereupon she swept the blankets and mattress off Sarah's bed, then Maggie's, then Eliza's, and was about to start on Lucy's when Lucy cried, "No! You mustn't!" and reached out to stop her.

The rest of us gaped, we were so taken aback, but that was nothing compared to what followed. Mrs. Staines demanded to know who Lucy thought she was, to tell *her* what she could or could not do — the very idea! She tore off Lucy's bedding and what did she discover, hidden between the folds of a blanket?

My handkerchief (but not the camas bulb), Annie's silver locket and Sarah's embroidered handkerchief.

Lucy was promptly hauled away with a number of questions flying after her, and all at the same time.
Where's my blue sash?
Do we still have to sleep on the floor?
What happened to Radish's carving?
Was it really you, Lucy?
How could you?
And where's my beaded necklace? (Maggie never mentioned she was missing a necklace. Maybe she didn't notice at first, since she has so many.)

Then we discussed why Lucy would have done such a thing.

Sarah said it was because Lucy wanted to have a few pretty things, having none of her own. That made me realize — tho' I am but speculating — it was *not* the camas Lucy was after, but the handkerchief. She must have wondered why I would have kept a *bulb,* but thought no more about it until Alec became ill and she remembered my story about the poison. She might have thrown out the bulb then, so as not to be caught with it, or maybe she threw it out from the start. It was not very pretty.

We reckoned that Mrs. Staines would have forgotten about us sleeping on the floor, so we pretended we'd heard her say yes to Sarah's question and remade the beds. Except for mine, since it was never unmade in the first place, being the one that comes after Lucy's.

Sunday, November 24th

Lucy's punishment was harsh. A caning, a week of Confinement (except for Sunday Service, School and meals), and a written apology to each person from whom she stole something.

And it was not because she wanted pretty things. It was Davy's idea, she told us, but Alec was involved too. They would get her to pilfer an item, hide it for a while and give it to them, whereupon they would trade it with the Indians. They suffered the same punishment as Lucy (but an extra-hard caning), and were ordered to retrieve the stolen items and return them to their owners.

We wanted to know why they hadn't used the items under Lucy's mattress. Was she keeping them for herself? Weren't they *good* enough? Had they been rejected?

No, it turned out that she took whatever she could whenever she had the chance, and gave the boys something when they needed it. "Because sometimes they used stuff of their own," she said, adding, "They traded the blue sash and the beaded necklace," as if Maggie would be pleased that her things might be considered valuable. "And Radish's carving."

So the sash I'd seen in the Songhees village *was* Maggie's.

I asked Lucy why she did what the boys told her to do, knowing it was wrong. She said it was a dare at first — she could not turn down a dare — and after that she couldn't refuse or else the boys would tell.

A few moments later she changed her story, saying it was Alec who'd gotten her involved, no one else, and she'd done it because Alec could be mean when she didn't do as he told her.

I'm not sure which version is the true one, but now that I think back to that day at the beach, the minute Alec told her to leave, she was ready to go. Maybe she is a little afraid of him. But no, it's more likely she doesn't want him to be mad at her, since he is the only family she has here.

She is exceedingly loyal to her brother, even if it means hurting her friends. It must make it difficult for her at times, choosing between the two.

Monday, November 25th

A month from today is Christmas. Nothing much happened last year at Fort Colvile, except for the flag being raised and having a special Dinner. It was the same at Fort Edmonton and I expect it will be the same here.

My favourite Christmas was in 1847, the year Mr.

Kane, the artist, was in Fort Edmonton on his way back from the West. There was fresh snow on the ground, everyone was dressed up, delicious smells were steaming out of every chimney — and Father was still alive. Who could have known it would turn out to be his last Christmas.

I remember that the officers and guests were having their Dinner at 2:00, after everyone else had eaten, and Suzanne and I snuck inside the dining hall and peeked through the doorway to spy — whereupon our jaws dropped to the floor!

The hall was huge and magnificent, especially now that I compare it to Fort Victoria's. No one believed me when I told them that the ceiling was decorated with gilt scrolls, so fancy that visitors gasped in awe the first time they went inside. Even Mr. Cavendish must have been agog! But on that Christmas Day, the magnificence of the hall was nothing compared to the feast!

Suzanne and I could only gape. Boiled buffalo hump, roast wild goose, white fish browned in buffalo marrow, buffalo tongue, beavers' tails, piles of potatoes and turnips and bread, and a dish we could not recognize but which Father later described as a boiled buffalo calf removed from its mother before birth. Everyone at the table had a job to do — serving, carving or dishing out — Father at the roast goose, someone else at the buffalo hump, Mr. Kane serving up helpings of moose nose, my favourite treat — it was a wonder I did not rush in and tear the plate away!

At one point Father looked over, caught my eye and frowned — whereupon Suzanne and I decided to leave. A good thing, for we might have fainted from hunger if we had stayed longer, even tho' we had already had our own Dinner. It was special too, with some of the same fare given to the officers, but nowhere near the abundance or variety.

Later that afternoon I visited Nokum. She had prepared the dried moose nose for the officers, and had tucked some inside her pouch especially for me.

Dear Nokum! I miss her and Father with an ache that is wider than the prairie. I miss the taste of moose nose and buffalo marrow and buffalo ribs roasted in the fire. I miss the big sky and the brilliance of the stars, the ice on the river and freshly fallen snow.

The dormitory is quiet tonight. Most of the girls are asleep. It is almost time to blow out the candles, but first I am going to eat some of my pemmican. I need the taste of home — did I just write *home?* I still think of Fort Edmonton that way, even though I have been away a long time, and cannot go back.

Tuesday, November 26th

A coastal ship arrived from Fort Vancouver with a packet of mail, and I got a letter from Aunt Grace.

Mr. Cavendish gave it to me at Supper. He also had letters for James and Eliza. He smiled and made pleasant remarks and told us the rain should not go on much longer, for the spirit thermometer in his office is showing lower temperatures, and perhaps there will be snow and wouldn't that be a happy change, etc.

Aunt Grace wrote the letter on October 30th. A party had stopped in Fort Colvile a few days earlier, with mail from the Saskatchewan District, and there was a letter to her from Mr. Rowand. He had asked her to inform me of Nokum's death, thinking I was still in Fort Colvile. Aunt says she was saddened by the news, knowing how deeply I loved my grandmother, and she wished she were able to comfort me. (I wish the same, for hearing of Nokum's death a second time is making me cry.)

Aunt was ill through October, but I am not to worry or neglect my studies, for she is improving steadily. She ends the letter by saying how much she and Uncle Rory miss me, especially my "rambunctious spirit and lively chatter."

I couldn't help but smile at that. It must be exceedingly dull in Fort Colvile for Aunt Grace to miss my spirit and chatter — but she would not have said it if it were not true. It could be that she feels towards me the way I feel towards her — I miss her more than I could have imagined. The next time I write I will tell her so.

She received the letter I wrote in August, and says she and Uncle were pleased that I added their little gifts to my *cassette*. (Thank Heaven I have my handkerchief back, as I'd hate to tell her it was stolen.) She says it brought back memories of our journey through the Rockies and how, in spite of the hardships, we were able to laugh. (Who could help it, with Uncle Rory?)

Wednesday, November 27th

Mr. Cavendish was right about the change in weather. The water in our buckets froze overnight.

Thursday, November 28th

The mud bogs in the yard have frozen solid thanks to the cold weather, and we no longer have to slop through mud to go to the privy. But the wagon ruts are treacherous, like miniature hills and valleys, and hard as rock.

Tuesday, December 3rd

We got up to find six inches of snow, and Mr. C's spirit thermometer stands at 14 degrees Fahr. It feels like a prairie winter!

Mr. Cavendish checks the thermometer each and every day and records the temperature in the *Post*

Journal. Today he wrote *Severe cold*.

The sun is shining and our spirits have been rising, with talk of sledding down Beacon Hill or the embankment, and sleigh rides — the others have told me there is a sleigh in the Fort — and we are going to build snowmen, for the snow here is a wet heavy snow that packs and holds it shape. It does not flutter off like goose down.

Later

The snow *hurts* when it is packed into a ball and thrown at you. I will practise throwing snowballs and get even with the boys tomorrow.

Friday, December 6th

Mild weather, melted snow, the yard a mess of slush.

No chance of a sleigh ride.

Dr. Benson has been transferred to Fort Vancouver and a new doctor has come to take his place. He arrived by canoe from Fort Rupert. His name is Dr. Helmcken and he looks very nice. Handsome, too! I would make him a Hero if I had not already chosen Mr. Cavendish.

Saturday, December 7th

What a time we had last night! The officers in the Common Room were making such a ruckus we could not bear it. When Sarah suggested we pour water upon them, everyone agreed, and I was elected to do it. (They have accepted me now as someone who is not afraid of misbehaving or paying the consequences — I suppose since I am accustomed to doing both.)

I protested at first (tho' weakly, for I was as sleepy and vexed as anyone) by saying, "But Mr. Cavendish is below. What if the water falls on *his* head?"

Lucy said we would wait until he was out of range, which would not take long, the way the men were clowning about.

Clowning is the word, for they were hopping about like horses and yelling, "Hurrah for the cavalry!"

We had a good laugh. Grown men and *officers* playing horses — they were worse than the boys! But enough was enough and down went the water on top of their heads.

The water ended the stomping but not the racket, for they switched to singing instead.

I suppose we must have slept a little.

Sunday, December 8th

Mr. Cavendish complimented us on our singing this a.m. and praised Mrs. Staines for training such an accomplished choir. She *blushed!* (We *all* did.)

When we lead the singing we have to face the congregation and, though I *try* not to gaze at Mr. Cavendish, my eyes manage to stray in his direction. If he meets my gaze, he smiles. I think it improves my singing.

The other girls talk about how he smiles at them, but I do not mind. I have no interest in him as a husband, only as the Hero in my Novel.

Since Mr. Cavendish's arrival I have looked forward to Sundays, and sometimes wish they would come more often.

Wednesday, December 25th

A holiday!

Rev. Staines held a Christmas Service after Breakfast and we played the rest of the morning. At Dinner we had venison and plum pudding and Christmas cake and candy. In the evening Rev. Staines and Mrs. Staines had a little party for us in their apartment, and we sang and played charades.

1851

Wednesday, January 1st

The New Year began with a gun salute and up went the flag — I could picture the same being done in Fort Edmonton and Fort Colvile and in hundreds of other posts — a resounding fanfare welcoming the New Year throughout the land.

I thought of Aunt Grace and Uncle Rory this morning, how Uncle would be going into the dining hall with the men and the officers to present themselves to the Chief Factor and receive their regale of cakes and rum and extra rations, and after that, another salute would let the women know it was their turn.

It was no different here, and Lucy and I went over to the hall and watched through the window, until we got cold and went back to the dormitory.

We had a special Dinner and played games all afternoon and now we have to get ready for the dance. It's in the dining hall, and Mrs. Staines has said we may go.

Thursday, January 2nd

We had a grand time last night, by turns dancing, singing and tapping our toes along with the fiddler.

Everyone at the Fort was there, or so it seemed, men and officers, women and children, and there was much laughing and talking, mostly in French, and Mr. Cavendish made a few of the older girls exceedingly happy by dancing with them.

I probably could have danced jigs and reels till midnight if Mrs. Staines hadn't herded us off by nine o'clock — and just as my favourite, "Belle Rosalie," was beginning! Suzanne and I loved that dance, everyone in a circle with their hands joined, one man singing, the others repeating, line after line, and at the last two lines the leader put "Belle Rosalie" into the centre (I think it was the person to his right) and she had to choose someone and kiss him on the cheek, and then go back to the circle to the left of the leader. And so it went, round after round, a different Rosalie in the centre each time. Or "Beau Rosier," if the person was a man. I always chose Father when I was Belle Rosalie, and when he was Beau Rosier he would choose me! He would swing me off my feet and whirl me around

Oof! Sarah just threw her pillow at me! She says I have to stop humming "Belle Rosalie," as she's had the tune playing in her head all day long and is going mad.

Maggie says a good pillow whack on the head is what Sarah needs and now there are pillows flying in every direction.

What fun! Time to join in.

Wednesday, February 12, 1851

It has been a while since my last entry, and in that time there have been no Adventures, no cases of pilfering, no unkind remarks from the other girls, no unjust punishments or accusations, in fact, nothing much to write about at all. So I put my Journal away for the same reason I put it away before — because I do not want it to be a dull record of weather and activities and who said what, or what we ate for Supper. That would be of no use in my future Novel. And I do not want to run out of pages in case something thrilling *does* happen.

But I have missed writing in my Journal, so have picked it up again.

We had two light snowfalls in the middle of January but the snow did not last. Mostly the weather has been the same as it was in November. Mild, rainy and grey with clouds of gloom. And *stormy* at times, with the wind blowing terrifically all night, all day — I swear for weeks on end. One day we had snow, hail, rain and the wind blowing a hurricane from dawn till dusk. What was there to do but schoolwork?

Sometimes we heard loud drumming coming from the Songhees village — a winter celebration, I suppose. It sounded thrilling and I longed to paddle over to see what it was about, but could find no way to do so. I have not seen Kwetlal for several weeks.

Saturday, February 22nd

A gift of a day — so fine it feels like spring. So with Journal in hand, I have come outside to bask in the sun.

How different it must be in Fort Edmonton today! Suzanne may be off on her showshoes or fighting a blizzard or making moccasins — or a less enjoyable task like scrubbing the floor of their quarters — and maybe thinking about me. She would have a hard time believing that I am sitting outside on a winter's day.

Tuesday, March 11th

Last week we went out on the *Beaver.* She was returning from Fort Langley with a load of salmon for the Sandwich Islands, and after the kegs had been unloaded and reloaded onto another ship, the captain took us on an excursion. The unloading lasted over a day, so by the time we got on board we were in a feverish state of excitement, especially the girls, because it was an excursion for the whole school, not just the boys.

I had seen the *Beaver* before, on her way to and from the forts along the coast, and I had heard the steam whistle from a distance, but to be on board was a new experience — and a noisy one! The hissing of steam, right in your ear, made the ship sound like a screeching, wheezing monster! To add to the ruckus, the Fort's cannon were fired, and the *Beaver* fired its own guns — all that fanfare, and just for us!

We steamed out of the harbour and into the strait as far as Esquimalt and then returned to the Fort. The ship has two masts with rigging, in case she runs out of steam, but she did not, and nor did we!

After that it was back to school.

Wednesday, March 19th

Bright green stalks have been shooting up in the gardens and the days are getting warmer. Spring comes so early here.

Monday, March 24th

Another letter from Aunt Grace, this one with the most exciting and surprising news! She and Uncle Rory are expecting a baby in May and they're moving to Vancouver's Island! Uncle Rory has been posted to the Company's new farm in Esquimalt, as blacksmith — mostly making nails, Aunt says, for all the new buildings that are planned — but he does not take on his duties until after the farm's bailiff arrives from England.

She closes by saying that she and Uncle miss me greatly, and await "the day of our reunion" as eagerly as the arrival of their "wee bairn."

Aunt Grace, a mother — I am thrilled with the news!

What sounds better — Aunt Jenna or Auntie Jenna?

I'll ask Lucy and the others for their advice.

Oh, and a newcomer to the Fort brought the letter. His name is Mr. Hammond and he was in Fort Colvile a few weeks ago. When Aunt Grace and Uncle Rory heard he was coming to Fort Victoria, Aunt asked him to give me the letter. She told him that I was one of the "brightest young ladies at the Staines School."

Aunt Grace, bragging! But in this case I forgive the Misdemeanor.

Later

No need to decide between Aunt or Auntie Jenna. Maggie rightly pointed out that since Aunt Grace is not my sister, her baby will be my cousin. I was crestfallen — until Sarah said I could still be called Aunt, being so much older. (But not *that* much older.)

Tuesday, March 25th

I was so excited about Aunt's news that I did not write a word about Mr. Hammond, and there is much to write, for he is an Artist, and has been travelling across the continent making sketches of forts,

Indians, etc. like Mr. Kane did. Mr. Kane was a magnificent artist. The first time he was at Fort Edmonton (on his way to the West) he showed us some of his sketches and paintings, and I could not believe how lifelike they were. He could draw a person's face with such detail, you would think you were looking at the actual person — why, you could read the expression in their eyes! As for their clothing, he did a portrait of one of the older girls at the Fort, and the way he showed the beadwork on her tunic — you could count every bead! Suzanne and I begged him to draw us, but he did not. Nokum said we would never have been able to sit still long enough.

He asked Nokum if he could do *her* portrait but she said no, she could not sit still either. I wish she had said yes.

He sketched old people, young people, men and women, Indians and whites (but mostly Indians), buffalo and horses, and little things, like cooking pots and Cree pipe-stems. He even sketched a buffalo *hunt* — and no one was sitting still then! He could draw scenes around a fort or a river or an Indian encampment and make you feel as if you were there.

Mr. Kane was interested in *everything* about the prairie and its people — but not just the prairie, the whole continent. According to Father, Governor Simpson sent a letter to all the Company officers saying that they had to give Mr. Kane free transportation on Company boats and free hospitality at all the posts.

I wonder where Mr. Kane is now? He was on his return trip from the Pacific Coast the Christmas he stopped at Fort Edmonton. I just realized — he probably visited Fort Victoria!

Oh fiddle, I was writing about Mr. *Hammond*, not Mr. Kane.

Well Mr. Hammond is from England. He is as friendly and handsome as Mr. Cavendish, tho' not as dashing, and the older girls have been quite charmed by his manner. Now there are endless arguments over which of the two would make the better husband. Lucy and I listen avidly and sometimes weigh in with our opinions. So far Mr. Cavendish is the favourite.

Mr. Hammond has been making sketches of trees and plants as well as preserving leaves and flowers to take back to England. His collection of souvenirs will be outstanding by the time he leaves — unlike mine, for I lost interest after only a few weeks when one of my seashells began to smell, and then I threw everything out.

Later

I've heard that a ship from England is arriving in May or June with new settlers for the Colony, new employees for the Company and new supplies, etc. The ship is called the *Tory*. People are already excited, and the carpenters and other workers have started to put up new buildings and to make furniture — oh, I just thought of something! That could be the ship that's bringing the bailiff for Esquimalt Farm! And after that, Uncle Rory, Aunt Grace and the wee bairn will arrive. My family.

Wednesday, March 26th

A group of us went to Beacon Hill yesterday and we came across Mr. Hammond sketching the landscape. We gathered round to see his work, and he told us about the route he had followed to Fort Victoria. It turns out it's the same route I took last June — by horseback from Fort Colvile to Fort Hope and by canoe to Fort Langley. Then he came to Fort Victoria but on the *Mary Dare* with its load of salmon. Everything he owns smells of salmon, he says.

Perhaps Mr. Hammond will be the Hero in my Novel. He has an adventurous life and is not bound by the HBCo to go here or there.

It is a beautiful time of year for Mr. Hammond to be here. Many plants and bushes are already in blossom, trees are in bud and the evergreen needles are beginning to show off their bright yellow-green tips.

Later

I found out that Mr. Kane was indeed in Fort
Victoria, four years ago this spring. The older Douglas girls recalled his visit to Fort Vancouver, where
they were living at the time, and said he left that
fort for Vancouver's Island. I wonder if Kwetlal and
Jimmy remember him, for he certainly would have
visited their village. Perhaps he sketched their grandmother.

Thursday, March 27th

A *hurricane* is blowing as I write — it threatens to
blow down the Fort if not the surrounding forest —
we are in the dormitory, shivering with fright. The
shrieks of wind, pelting rain, the crash of falling tim-
ber, the thumps of blowing branches as they hit

Damus! Wind blew out my candle.

Friday, March 28th

A wonderful day in school, for Mrs. Staines invited Mr. Hammond to give us some drawing lessons.
He was patient and encouraging and, as a result, we
worked harder than usual and our drawings were the
better for it. Mrs. Staines said so herself.

He is a good artist but not as good as Mr. Kane.

Last night was one of the worst for boisterous behaviour, but a splendid night for Spying, so Lucy and I lifted the loose floorboard between our beds and invited the others to join us. The men would have been amused if they had looked up and seen us peering down at them, but they were too occupied to bother.

They were telling jokes and stories about the time they were here or there or some other place and what happened to so-and-so, and guffawing and trying to outdo each other with spectacular tales of adventure, and they were roasting oysters on the stove and drinking and smoking their pipes while we kept nudging each other for a chance to view the revelry.

Then someone decided that Mr. Cavendish had had way too much to drink and had to be sobered up. "Let's give him a tossing!" he shouted.

The others agreed with no end of hearty-har-hars. They put Mr. Cavendish on top of a blanket — he was laughing as much as anyone — and four men each took a corner and threw him into the air! They ignored his cries for mercy and kept tossing him until the poor man promised he would never touch another drop. (He was still laughing, but somewhat weakly.)

The party calmed down after that, but our party

was just beginning, for Lucy decided it would be fun to have our own tossing. She volunteered to go first and we took turns after that, tossing and being tossed — until our arms were worn out and we were giddy from laughing.

I enjoy being with the other girls, now that they have accepted me and my "outlandish behaviour" (as Sarah calls it, tho' with a note of admiration). It may be because I have spent more time with them since the New Year, instead of wandering off on my own, and we have therefore come to know one another better. And ever since the night Lucy confided in me about missing her mother, she and I have been friends.

Almost time for Service. I wonder how the officers will look after such a night. Mr. Douglas insists on *everyone* being at Service regardless of what might have happened the night before.

Monday, March 31st

Rev. Staines took everyone on a Nature Walk to Beacon Hill after Dinner and we went by way of the new footbridge at the head of the Bay. Mr. Douglas had it built, because he is building a house across the Bay and the footbridge makes it easier for his workmen to reach the site. Now it takes less time to reach Beacon Hill and saves us a good part of the muddy trail — except we miss the excitement of balancing on the plank to cross the stream. Not that we *have* to use the footbridge.

We saw clusters of wildflowers blooming in the woods and oak groves, and Rev. Staines told us their names — bluebells, purple shooting stars and white fawn lilies. And in the meadows, the green shoots of camas. They're not yet in flower, but the buds should be opening soon.

Friday, April 4th

The boys are in a high state of excitement for they think we are at war with the Songhees.

Alec and Davy heard this from Mr. Beauchamp who heard it from a worker at the dairy who saw an Indian kill one of the Company's cows, and once Mr. Douglas heard of it he sent a message to the Songhees Chief demanding that the man responsible present himself at the Fort to be punished and, if he fails to come on his own, the Chief must bring him. According to the boys, Mr. Douglas said that an example must be made, for such acts will not be tolerated.

Alec and Davy burst into the schoolroom with the news and got everyone riled up, the other boys weighing in with what *they* had seen and heard — muskets being cleaned, cannonballs stacked, etc. — all of it made up, or greatly exaggerated, I think, for I would have recounted such a story in much the same way.

Whether he believed the boys or not, Rev. Staines found the topic so interesting he gave up on Latin and launched into a lesson on Justice, saying a man had to be harsh and show who had the upper hand, and when he was a student at Cambridge . . .

At that point I stopped listening and thought of a Plot for my Novel — how something minor could grow into a skirmish, or even a full-fledged war, with Dire Consequences.

Later

I was in the yard after Supper, hoping to learn more about "the War," and saw Jimmy. He was standing at the side of Bachelors' Hall. I did not actually see him at first, as he was somewhat in shadow, and when he spoke my name I jumped in alarm.

He looked so anxious, I thought that something must have happened to Kwetlal, but he shook his head when I mentioned her name, and gave me to understand that it was the Fort that made him uneasy. It was the first time he had set foot inside the gate. I was surprised at this, since he sometimes transported the officers here and there (or whoever else wanted to hire a canoe), but I gathered from what he said that his uncle or father made the arrangements, and he waited on the beach.

I was also surprised he was let in without being stopped and questioned, but he said that no one appeared to notice. Perhaps because the watchman was occupied.

He had been waiting for me with a message. His grandmother had a gift for me and could I go to the village?

I told him I could be at Laurel Point the next morning.

I wonder what she has for me. I must give her something in return.

Saturday, April 5th

I am confined to the dormitory, but do not mind, for there is much to record and I can do so without interruption.

I met Jimmy this morning as planned and we paddled across to the village. Kwetlal had been gathering seaweed, but when we reached the beach she stopped and went with us to the lodge.

Her grandmother was seated in front of her loom, weaving a blanket with mountain-goat wool and dog wool. She stopped when I arrived and, after we exchanged greetings, she opened a large cedar box and removed a small folded blanket. She handed it to me, indicating that it was a gift for me, a friend from far away over the mountains. (I think that's what she meant.)

I was overwhelmed, and considered it a great honour to receive such a gift. It has a beautiful design of stripes and zigzags in red, white, tan and brown, and was woven not only with goat and dog wool but with cedar bark.

In return I gave her my deerskin pouch, the one Nokum had made and decorated with porcupine quills. My eyes welled up as I was handing it to her, and I let her know, by pointing to Kwetlal and then back to her, that my grandmother had made it and now she was dead, and I put my hands over my heart to show how much I had loved her. This needed no telling in words.

Oh, how hard it was to give it up! I keep wondering if I should have kept it, if it was too precious to give away — even for something as valuable as a dog-wool blanket. But Kwetlal's grandmother has been kind to me, and I am grateful.

Well I had put some pemmican into the pouch, and explained as best I could how it was made, and how it would give her energy and strength and last for many years. It took a long time, especially when I tried to describe the buffalo.

The porcupine was even more difficult! And as for describing how it defends itself with its quills — well I finally took a sharp splinter of cedar, pricked it into my skin and yelped! Oh, how it hurt! And how they laughed!

We were enjoying the game of charades, and I was thinking what else I could describe when Jimmy appeared and said it was time to go. He was agitated about something — Kwetlal noticed too, for she gave me a nervous look — and I began to fear the worst, especially when he picked up his harpoon.

We left in a hurry but had scarcely taken two steps when the commotion began.

Men were coming from all directions, shouting, whooping and running towards the beach. Their faces were painted and they were armed, with axes and knives and harpoons and fishing poles — the long ones they use for herring, with the sharp spears at the end — and some of the men had muskets. Jimmy ran to join them, and Kwetlal and I followed, keeping well off to the side.

When we got to the edge of the village we saw two Company boats approaching the shore, the men armed with muskets.

I could not believe my eyes. We were going to war because of a cow?

The men in the nearest boat looked ready to jump into the water and storm ashore, but the Songhees had their weapons pointed straight at them and before the Company men could make a move, the Songhees rushed into the water and seized the muskets! Whereupon there was a bit of a set-to, but nothing serious that I could make out, and by then the second boat had gotten closer. The man standing in the bow was waving a pistol and yelling at his men to charge or do something, but they stayed in the boat looking nervous.

By that time the oarsmen had turned the first boat around and those in the second were hard at it to do the same — but as it was turning, the man at the bow looked in my direction and I recognized Dr. Helmcken.

Once the Company men had rowed across, Jimmy paddled me to the Point and I walked hastily back to the Fort with one thought in mind — had Dr. Helmcken seen me? Would he tell Mrs. Staines? Would I fret for hours, wondering if she knew and when she would confront me? I decided to save her the trouble by confessing.

I told her I had gone to the village, knowing it was forbidden, because she would not have given me permission had I asked. And I *had to* go, out of politeness, for I had received an invitation. I even showed her the beautiful gift I had received. I told her I was sorry if I had upset her, and would confine myself to the dormitory for

Time to Spy! There is movement afoot down below!

Later

I cannot believe what has happened! To think that I have spent months exploring beyond the stockade in search of Adventure, only to find it *directly* under my nose! I am in a Delirium of Excitement — not the happy or thrilling sort, but the dizzying, heart-sinking-with-dread sort that is churning my stomach in a wretched way — for I have uncovered a Despicable Crime, committed by a Real-Life Villain. *Mr. Cavendish is a Murderer!*

My Spying is no longer the game I once thought it to be, but an act that has thrown me into a mess of problems and secrets and I do not know whether to keep the knowledge to myself or to tell someone, but who? If only Aunt Grace were here!

And if I *do* tell someone — Mrs. Staines, for instance — would she believe me? Would *anyone* believe me? Mr. Cavendish is an *officer,* everyone likes him and admires him, whereas I am only a schoolgirl, known to be reckless and wilful and inclined to exaggerate. And to admit that I have been Spying —

Or if I tell Lucy — no, I trusted her once before and it was a grave mistake

Mon dieu, did I just write *grave?*

I must calm myself. If I record the matter as faithfully as I can remember, I may see my way more clearly.

To begin, I heard movement below. It was early afternoon and, knowing that the girls were in Deportment Class and that I would not be disturbed, I knelt down at my secret Spy Hole and saw that Mr. Cavendish was in his room. There was a knock on his door. Mr. Cavendish opened it and in came Mr. Hammond.

Mr. Cavendish greeted him in his usual hearty way. "Afternoon, Hammond! What can I do for you?"

Whereupon Mr. Hammond said, "Afternoon, Cavendish. Or should I say, *Collins?*"

There was a long tense silence as the men stared at one another. Finally Mr. Cavendish said, "How long have you known?"

"Not until this very moment," Mr. Hammond said. "Your answer has just confirmed my suspicion that you are in fact John Collins. The very John Collins who killed my cousin, Julia Lindsay."

His *cousin!* I was mesmerized — so caught up in the conversation, it was as if I were reading a Novel! But suddenly I stopped short. This was *real life!* Mr. Cavendish was somebody else! I was peering down at a *murderer!*

By then my heart was beating wildly. I felt anxious and afraid. I wanted to move away but did not, for fear of being discovered. So I stayed and listened — straining hard, for they had lowered their voices. I stayed until they had gone, and I have been writing in a fury ever since.

Here is what I have come to understand. Mr. Hammond's cousin Julia had been engaged to marry Mr. Cavendish but had broken her engagement because of his "excessive drinking" and "fits of jealous rage," and she had died *at his hands* not long afterwards. (Mr. H had produced one of her letters, and he read aloud the part about drinking and rages.) Mr. Cavendish swore it was an accident — he had been begging Miss Lindsay to reconsider when she had slipped and fallen down a flight of stairs. But Mr. Hammond said the courts would decide whether it was an accident or not. And Mr. Cavendish is also wanted in London for desertion from the Royal Navy — which would have been crime enough!

Mr. Hammond has been

Back to writing. Deportment Class is over, and Lucy and Eliza have come and gone. I heard them coming and remembered I had forgotten to replace the knot in the floor. So I raced to do that and covered it up, with only seconds to spare. We talked for a while and then they left. I was glad of the distraction, for I was in quite a state, and feel the same now, but I have to continue before I forget everything.

I gathered from the men's conversation that Mr. Hammond had been "abroad" during his cousin's involvement with Mr. Cavendish, and had learned of him only through her letters. Another one of the parts he read out loud was a heart-wrenching plea for Nigel (Mr. Hammond's name) to hurry home, as she was growing "ever more fearful of Mr. Cavendish's violent temper." I think those were the words, or close enough.

By the time Mr. Hammond received the letter and

got back to London, it was too late. He learned what he could and has been tracking Mr. Cavendish for months. And now he means to have him arrested.

But Mr. Cavendish just laughed at that idea, saying things like "no proof" and "your word against mine," and Mr. Hammond said nothing.

I wish I had told Lucy and Eliza, even if it meant revealing the Spy Hole, because then I would not be on my own. But would they believe me? They'd laugh! Mr. Cavendish, a murderer with a violent temper? It cannot be true.

Sunday, April 6th

When I am talkative and energetic I am scolded for not being quiet and still. Today was the opposite. I kept to myself and spoke to no one. At one point Lucy said, "Are you ill? You're not bouncing or humming."

At Service this morning, I listened intently to Rev. S's sermon, hoping that his words might carry a message or give me an inkling of what I should do, but they did not.

At the end of the Service, as we were filing out, Mr. Cavendish caught my eye and smiled. But instead of smiling back as I normally do, I turned away, my face hot and my heart beating painfully. Now I have a new cause for worry. Does he *know* I was listening? Did he catch sight of me at the Spy

Hole? Was his smile a *warning*? Did my turning away so rudely tell him I had something to hide, that I can back Mr. Hammond's word? Does he know that I know?

I am ill with speculation.

And where is Mr. Hammond? I've not seen him all day.

Later

Mr. Cavendish *did not* raise his eyes to the ceiling while I was Spying, not once. I would have noticed if he had, so of course he did not see me.

Monday, April 7th

After Dinner I spoke to Mrs. Staines in private. I asked what one should do if they knew something about someone, or if they heard something — I should have rehearsed what I meant to say, for it came out in such a muddle that she stopped me and said, "I don't follow you, Jenna. Speak plainly."

I had scarcely started my second attempt when Rev. Staines came into the classroom with Radish and Thomas by the ears and demanded that they confess to Mrs. Staines whatever it was they had done.

I slipped out without being noticed.

I am at my wit's end with worry and frustration. Why hasn't Mr. Hammond at least tried to have Mr. Cavendish arrested? Maybe he has, and nothing

A few moments ago Lucy burst in to tell me that a group of Songhees, including the Chief, have come into the yard and they're talking to Mr. Douglas, and they've all got muskets, and if I want to know what's happening I'd better get outside.

Maybe in a while, I told her, and pleaded a headache.

She gave me a puzzled look — no doubt thinking, How unlike Jenna — but went off without asking questions.

I think I already know what's happening. The Songhees are here to make some sort of payment for the cow, and to return the muskets they took from the men in the boats — *mon dieu*, was it only two days ago?

Tuesday, April 8th

At Breakfast I learned that I was right about the Songhees' visit. At least some matters can be resolved.

I came back to the dormitory after Breakfast, and lay down with my special wool blanket.

Lucy came in and asked what was wrong. I told her I did not feel like going to School and, if Mrs. Staines questioned my absence, Lucy could tell her whatever she liked.

Within an hour Mrs. Staines appeared at my bedside. "You look well enough for a girl who's been bitten by a spider and come down with malaria."

Lucy's excuse for my absence was so unexpected I would have laughed had I not felt so miserable. "What is the real reason?" Mrs. Staines said, and the grilling began.

Was I ill? No.

Was my aunt ill? No.

Was there something troubling me? No.

Had someone hurt me in some way? No.

She knew there was something, but there was little she could do except order me to go to School. She said I would feel better if I concentrated on my lessons.

"Yes," I said, but stayed where I was.

She tried again, said that everyone knew I was a "determined young lady," but even the strongest needed assistance sometimes and I should not be too proud to admit it. Her parting words: "You no longer have to prove your mettle."

I wish I could have told her the truth. Her face showed concern and, by calling me *determined* rather than *stubborn* or *pig-headed* (names she has used in the past) she seemed to be taking me seriously. Otherwise I would be sitting in class with a twisted ear.

She was wrong about one thing, for I *do* have to prove my mettle. If this were my Novel, my Heroine would not hesitate, she would go bravely forth and do the right thing — she would not be cowering in her room *writing* about what she ought to do.

Wednesday, April 9th

I *have* to stop this cowering and *tell* someone, but I *cannot,* because I am afraid of being punished for Spying or accused of lying and I'm afraid of Mr. Cavendish. Somehow he knows that I overheard his conversation with Mr. Hammond — I'm sure of it — because yesterday when I passed him in the yard he said, "Off for a walk, Jenna? Be careful in the woods. Accidents happen. We would not want you to get hurt." I'm certain he was warning me to keep quiet.

Has he warned Mr. Hammond? Or *threatened* him? He might think Mr. Hammond really does have proof. That must be why Mr. Hammond hasn't told Mr. Douglas, because he's afraid —

Where is Mr. Hammond? Someone said he hired some paddlers and went up the coast to Sooke Inlet to do some sketching, but he should have been back by now — it is not *that* far, only 23 miles from here. Is he not worried that Mr. C will run away somewhere? What if Mr. Cavendish has murdered Mr. Hammond?

This would make a fine Plot —

Oh I am so ashamed, how can I even *think* of a Plot at such a time? I always thought of Adventure as a Journey with *Excitement* at every turn, not *real* Danger, and not something that involved *Murder* — that was for Novels. I never thought that a Villain could exist in Real Life, and I never imagined that a Villain could be someone I liked. Mr. Cavendish was meant to be my Hero!

It is now time for Dinner but I'm not hungry. I'll eat some pemmican and go to my Lookout and I will stay there until I get enough courage to tell someone, even if it takes all afternoon. If I happen to see Mr. Hammond — and I pray that I do — I'll tell him what I know and we can go to Mr. Douglas together. As long as Mr. Cavendish does not try to stop us.

Monday, April 14th

Five days since my last entry and much has happened. If I were writing a Novel, this chapter would be called:

In which Jenna Survives a most Thrilling and Dangerous Adventure, aided by some Unlikely Heroes, including one Edward Radisson Lewis otherwise known as Radish

Where was the body? Jenna had to find it — for without the body, justice could not prevail! And where to begin her search? Where else, but at the scene of the crime!

Her body trembled as she was leading her companions through the meadow, for she could not prevent the details of the horrific scene from flooding into her mind.

The Lookout! High in the cedar, from where, horror-stricken, she had witnessed the grisly attack, unable to utter a sound!

The boulder, not far from the tree, where an unsuspecting Mr. Hammond had been sketching the majestic mountains across the strait!

The spot where the forest trail opened onto the meadow, and the stealthy appearance of the villainous Mr. Cavendish!

The knife in his hand, its steel blade gleaming with menace!

His cowardly attack on Mr. Hammond — sneaking up from behind and viciously stabbing him in the back of his neck until the blood spurted forth and he was stone cold dead!

Jenna looked at the blood-splattered boulder and remembered the deep swoon she had fallen into on witnessing the grisly murder and how, an hour later, she had come to her senses to find herself still in her Lookout, cradled by the protective branches of the cedar.

But wait! What was this? On looking down from the tree, having steeled herself for the sight of Mr. Hammond's lifeless body, she was shocked to discover that *his body was gone!* She had swung down from the tree, raced to the Fort and gathered her stalwart companions.

"We must search the woods!" she cried. "Leave no stone unturned!"

They fanned off into the woods, crawling through the dense underbrush, climbing over fallen trees, growing ever discouraged as an ominous purple twilight bore down upon them. And at last, when all seemed lost, Radish, the smallest and youngest of the group, cried out, "Eureka!"

He had found the corpse of Mr. Hammond!

The handsome, talented, adventurous, *honourable* Mr. Hammond! To have come so far to seek justice for the death of his beloved cousin, only to find himself cut down in the prime of his life by a Villain, and his body stuffed inside a hollow log. Such an inglorious and undeserving end!

Jenna seethed with rage and loathing. How dare the odious Mr. Cavendish betray the fondness and admiration she had placed

Damus interruptus!

Radish has just come in and asked if I've finished my chapter. I haven't, but I'll read what I've written so far and see if he likes it.

Later

Radish liked the chapter, especially the part about him, and he is thrilled that I used his real name in the title. His only complaint was the word *Eureka,* but when I explained it is a famous Greek word (not Latin) that means "I found it," he was content. He plans to use it in class to impress Rev. Staines.

Tuesday, April 15th

In which Jenna Records the Facts in a Manner Befitting a Post Journal

I keep hearing Aunt Grace: "Keep to the facts! Life is not a Novel!"

Indeed it is not.

The chapter I read to Radish is for my Novel. It is not a true account.

The true facts are these:
1. I was up in my Lookout.
2. I saw Mr. Cavendish attack Mr. Hammond.
3. I screamed and fell out of the tree.

Here are the details:

I was sitting in my Lookout, thinking of Nokum and what she would have done in my situation, when who should come into view but Mr. Hammond. I was so relieved to see him! He crossed the meadow, sat down on the boulder and opened his sketchbook. I was about to climb down and talk to him when I saw Mr. Cavendish creeping out of the woods behind Mr. Hammond with a knife in his hand.

My heart leapt into my throat. I tried to utter a warning but no sound came out. So I summoned my strength and courage and every bit of mettle — as well as my *fury* at Mr. Cavendish — and screamed, *"Mr. Hammond!"*

Well the cry came out so forcefully that I lost my balance. I caught a glimpse of the two men struggling, but could not say who had the upper hand — and though I fought hard to stay on the branch, I could not, and down I fell.

Mr. Hammond brought me back, senseless, to the Fort. Later I learned that my scream had alerted him to danger, and he had turned in time to ward off the attack. Mr. Cavendish fled.

Some time later I woke up in the dormitory with a broken *ulna* — a Latin word that Dr. Helmcken taught me, which means forearm. He straightened it and put on padded splints. I tried to be brave and pretend that it didn't hurt, but it did. Fortunately it's my left arm so I can still write. Dr. Helmcken said I was lucky the tree was bushy because the branches helped to break my fall.

We are still in shock regarding the villainous Mr. Cavendish. When Mr. Hammond related what had happened, a party was immediately sent out to seize the Villain. He was found the next day on a beach a few miles up the coast and taken to the Bastion. He will be a prisoner there until the next Royal Navy ship arrives, likely in June. Then he will be taken to London and tried for desertion and for the murder of Julia Lindsay, and for his attempted attack on Mr. Hammond.

Mr. Hammond will be going too. I almost wish he would take me, so I could see London and go to the trial and give what he called "corroborative testimony." At least my words will be there to back him up, for he is taking the report that I had to write. A true and factual account of everything I had seen and heard, from start to finish. I wanted to say that Mr. Cavendish was a despicable creature, a Villain who hid his wickedness behind the face of a Hero and deserved to be sent to the gallows — but I had to write without a single embellishment. It is what they call a "Sworn Statement" and will be read by important people in a Court of Law.

Before I came to write the account I had to go to Mr. Douglas's office and tell what had happened. All the important people of the Fort were there, like Mr. Douglas of course, and Mr. Finlayson and Dr. Helmcken. Mr. Hammond was there too. I answered a lot of questions and everything was recorded, questions and answers. There were more than a few raised eyebrows when I confessed that everything I'd seen and heard had been through a Spy Hole or from a tree. I could feel Mrs. Staines' frown without even looking in her direction.

This whole affair may be useful in a Novel sometime, but I would change the names of the characters and add more episodes. And I would have my Hero go to London to testify.

Mr. Hammond says I'm a true Hero for saving his life. It makes me laugh, because Heroes go into the unknown and have thrilling Adventures. They do not fall out of trees.

Wednesday, April 16th

The Fort is abuzz with sawing and hammering and no end of activity — over 20 new buildings going up, with more in the outlying farms — all to accommodate the employees who are due to arrive next month. There is a new dwelling house, a bakery, a flour mill and goodness knows what else.

My arm feels much better. Dr. Helmcken says it is healing as it should.

Thursday, April 17th

I have been the centre of attention since all this happened and, though I enjoyed it at first, I am becoming weary of telling the same story over and over again. And the questions! At School, at meals, in the Dormitory, in the yard. How did you know about Mr. Cavendish? Where is your secret Spy Hole? Is that why you were behaving strangely? What were you doing in a tree? Where is the tree? Do you really have a Lookout in the tree? How did you feel when you saw the knife in Mr. Cavendish's hand? Tell us again!

Radish's favourite question: What would have happened if Mr. Cavendish had killed Mr. Hammond *after* you had cried out?

And his answer: You would be dead, wouldn't you, Jenna?

I try not to think about that.

Everyone wanted to see the Spy Hole and the tree. The boys climbed up the tree but could not find the Lookout. I didn't tell them it was only a branch.

Saturday, April 19th

I walked to Beacon Hill and saw where the men are clearing land. In one area they are felling oaks and removing brush and, in another, they are ploughing under a field of camas. The camas is almost in full bloom, and the sight of the men and plough-horse trampling all over it made me so angry I shouted, "You can't plough there! It's camas!"

"And what might that be?" says one of the men.

I could tell from his mocking tone that he was not taking me seriously, but nonetheless I told him about the Songhees eating the camas bulbs the way we eat potatoes. "It's a *crop*," I said, becoming more and more heated. "They harvest it! You're plough-ing up their garden!"

He scoffed, as did the others, and after telling me to take it up with Mr. Douglas, went back to work. 400 bushels of potatoes they had to plant, once the land was ploughed.

I feel badly for Kwetlal and her family. There are acres of meadow left, but every time one is ploughed up, the camas that grew there is gone.

Monday, April 21st

Last night I saw a fearsome dark shape standing in the doorway, peering into the room to see which bed was mine, creeping towards me — and I started to scream.

Lucy got out of bed and shook me awake.

"Mr. Cavendish!" I gasped. "He's escaped from the Bastion. He's coming to get me! Did you see him?"

By then Mrs. Staines was at my side, telling me it

was a dream and that Mr. Cavendish was locked up securely, and there was no need to be afraid.

"Are you sure?" I kept asking her. "He hasn't escaped?"

She assured me that all was well.

I will not feel at ease until he is on the ship and sailing back to England.

Thursday, April 24th

Another nightmare.

If this were a Novel I would have my Heroine deliver to Mr. Cavendish a plate of jam tarts. He would say, "Lovely," and eat every one — not knowing, until it was too late, that they were abundantly laced with tartar emetic.

Friday, April 25th

In another month or so Aunt Grace and Uncle Rory will be parents! Will my little cousin be a boy or a girl? I cannot wait to see the "wee bairn!"

Saturday, April 26th

I am sitting in the meadow, eating a little pemmican and feasting on a shimmering carpet of blue camas, a deep violet-blue that flows in every direction, over and beyond Beacon Hill, with clusters of yellow buttercups and chocolate lilies, and millions of butterflies dipping in and out amongst the flowers. Thank Heaven the men have not ploughed under *all* the meadows, for it truly is a glorious sight.

Later

I was walking back to the Fort, along the forest trail, when I heard a noise behind me. I whirled around to confront the culprit, fearing that it was Mr. Cavendish, but who should it be but Lucy, Radish and Alec. They had followed me to the meadow to make sure I was all right.

"Because if Cavendish *did* break out of jail," says Alec, "you might have needed our help."

"And what if you had another fall," says Radish, "and broke your other arm?"

"And you couldn't finish your Novel?" says Lucy.

"Don't be silly," I told them, but inside I was pleased.

Monday, April 28th

Another fine balmy day so I walked to the camas meadow after Dinner. Kwetlal and her family were there, clearing away weeds, and a few of the older women were separating out the white camas from the blue — an easy task, now that the plants are in flower. I watched how carefully they dug them right up by the roots and set them aside to be planted in another spot or destroyed.

I stayed on until it was time to go back to school.

Friday, May 2nd

This is the last page of my Journal.

I was hoping the end would correspond with something interesting — the arrival of the *Tory* or a picnic at Beacon Hill, a visit to the Songhees village or even the last day of School — but no. My Adventure Journal ends on a warm spring day with Breakfast (treacle, not jam), School, Dinner (salmon & potatoes), more School, Supper (potatoes & salmon) and now bed.

Oh, and in between School and Supper a group of us walked to Beacon Hill to admire the camas on the unploughed meadows.

Tomorrow I must go to the Trade Store and see about obtaining a new Journal, for I am anxious to begin a proper Novel. I am sure to have no end of new ideas.

I need to rethink *Adventure*. I have come to understand that in real life, an adventure can be a small thing. It can happen close to home, right under your nose. Perhaps it is not a journey or a heroic act, but a feeling. Or is it simply an idea?

Mrs. Staines is coming.

Time to blow out the candle.

Epilogue

Jenna's last two months at Staines School were marked by three significant events. The first, on May 9, 1851, was the arrival of the long-awaited ship the *Tory,* bringing a number of new employees and settlers for the colony. Among the passengers were six teenaged girls — five of whom were the daughters of Captain Langford, bailiff of the Company's Esquimalt Farm where Jenna would soon be making her home. The girls would eventually become friends.

The following month, on June 27, Jenna found herself on the Gallery watching Her Majesty's Ship the *Portland* sail into Esquimalt harbour. The *Portland* caused a great deal of excitement, for it was the flagship, the main ship of the entire HMS fleet — and when the Admiral hosted a ball and invited all the pupils of Staines School, the girls could not believe their good fortune. Jenna never forgot the thrill of boarding the enormous fifty-two–gun frigate and dancing to the music played by the ship's own band.

During the ball Jenna learned that Mr. Cavendish had been taken on board the *Portland* in chains and under armed guard, and would be made to stand trial when the ship returned to London. Mr. Hammond planned to return on the same ship, taking with him Jenna's written testimony.

The third and, to Jenna, the most significant event, was the arrival of Aunt Grace, Uncle Rory and her little cousin, Ann. By the end of June, the family was settled in their new quarters at Esquimalt Farm (named Colwood by Capt. Langford) and Jenna was more than eager to join them.

Jenna spent the summer of 1851 at Colwood Farm, becoming reacquainted with her aunt and helping her with the baby. There was a year's worth of experiences, thoughts and feelings to share, as well as a wedding to celebrate — for on July the 5th, to fulfill the promise they'd made in Fort Edmonton, Aunt Grace and Uncle Rory were married by Rev. Staines.

During the summer, however, Jenna was surprised to find herself missing school and wanting to go back. She had enjoyed her studies, in spite of the grumbling; she had grown to like the other girls, especially Lucy; she could still see Kwetlal and visit the village; and best of all, her family was now less than 5 miles away. With her aunt's approval, she subscribed to Staines School for another year and, though she lived there as a boarder, she went home to her family whenever she could.

In the early spring of 1852 Uncle Rory purchased 60 acres in Metchosin and set about clearing land to build a farmhouse. It was here that Jenna found herself that summer, and she would remain at Shady Creek Farm for the next five years.

She adored little Ann and the two boys who came after, and spent hours entertaining them with stories. They hung on her every word, especially the story of how she had saved the artist Mr. Hammond.

She settled into a routine of farm life with its multiple chores, but took time to enjoy an active social life. She had made friends with Martha Cheney who, like the Langford girls, had arrived on the *Tory* in 1851 and who, like Jenna, lived with her aunt and uncle in Metchosin, kept a diary and loved to go riding. As for the Langford girls, their father liked nothing better than to host parties and socials at Colwood, and Jenna was a frequent guest at their home.

For the Rev. and Mrs. Staines, their time in Fort Victoria did not end happily. The parson had become a vocal member of a group of colonists who complained vigorously about the HBC and James Douglas. In 1851 Douglas had been appointed the new Governor of Vancouver Island, but remained as Chief Factor of Fort Victoria, leaving the colonists to wonder whether he would treat them fairly — on such issues as land sales, for instance — or make decisions in favour of the Company. In 1854 Rev. Staines boarded a ship for London, taking a petition requesting that Parliament cancel the HBC's grant to Vancouver Island and replace it with free parliamentary institutions. The petition, written by Staines and signed by many officers, never reached London, for Staines drowned when his ship was hit by a storm not far off Vancouver Island. Mrs. Staines closed the school and, accompanied by her nephew Horace, moved back to England.

At a Christmas party in 1856, Jenna met Matthew Farris, the man who would later become her husband. The youngest son of a well-to-do English landowner, he had first come to Victoria in 1851 as an officer of the HBC vessel the *Norman Morison,* and had since made several sailings between Victoria and London. He had made his last voyage in the spring of 1855, and was seeking "a new adventure." Meanwhile, he was working as a Clerk at Fort Victoria.

Jenna had had many suitors during the previous three years and had turned down so many marriage proposals that Aunt Grace was constantly teasing her about being fussier than she herself had been. That changed with Matthew Farris. He and Jenna were married on Christmas Day, 1857.

Four months later, they were walking along Wharf Street below the fort when they saw a paddle-wheeler steaming into the harbour. There was nothing unusual about that, except that the decks of *this* particular vessel were crowded with men wearing the red flannel shirts of gold miners. "Gold in the Fraser River!" they were shouting. The Fraser River Gold Rush was on.

Jenna and Matt caught the excitement. This was the adventure they had been waiting for! In less than a month they were heading up the Fraser River to

Fort Yale, the gateway to the gold.

They panned for gold like thousands of others but, unlike thousands of others, were successful in staking a claim. They worked it for a year, sold it at a good profit and bought a hotel in Yale. Renamed the Wayfarer's Inn, it became a popular and hospitable place, and Jenna liked nothing better than talking to the miners and listening to their stories. Like the Saskatchewan River where she grew up, the Fraser flowed with stories, and Yale, like Fort Edmonton, was a place for comers and goers. Jenna never failed to give a hot meal and warm welcome to those passing through, or to wish them well on their journey.

Their numbers increased in 1862 with the discovery of gold in the Cariboo, and even more in 1865 with the completion of the Cariboo Wagon Road, the steep narrow road that linked the sternwheeler terminus at Yale to the gold-mining town of Barkerville, 400 miles away. For several years the Wayfarer's Inn never lacked for guests.

Jenna often felt that the attention she gave the miners helped take her mind off her own sorrow — the loss of three infants in the space of seven years. It didn't help to know that countless babies died before their first birthday, or that countless mothers grieved their loss as deeply as she did. Eventually she had three more children, Robert, John and Susannah, all of whom survived into adulthood. Robert's arrival on July 1, 1867, was doubly special, as it coincided with Canada's birth as a nation.

During her time in Yale, Jenna travelled to Fort Edmonton — a trip she had been longing to make for years. Her first sight of the prairie made her realize how much she had missed it, but it wasn't the same. There was scarcely a sign of buffalo, and most of the people she had known were gone.

Not so with Suzanne! Jenna found her childhood friend living on a farm with her husband and seven children a few miles east of the fort. The years disappeared in an instant. On seeing each other, Jenna and Suzanne were two high-spirited and adventurous girls again, talking, teasing, laughing and gossiping as if no time at all had passed. (Much to the delight of Suzanne's oldest daughter, who said she had never seen her mother so happy.)

Jenna also made several trips to Shady Creek Farm. Her young cousins greeted her visits with delight and were always eager to hear new stories. During one of her visits she overheard Ann telling a friend that Cousin Jenna had saved a man from being murdered by *"flying* from the top of a tree, knocking the villain to the ground and wrestling the knife from his hand!" Matt laughed when Jenna related this, saying that Ann had told him the same story when he was courting Jenna. Exaggeration, Jenna realized, appeared to be a family trait.

She loved to spend time with Aunt Grace and Uncle Rory, and was surprised to discover how much she and her aunt actually had in common.

Whenever possible, the family, or one of the cousins, would return with her to Yale for a holiday, or to help out in the inn. They were much loved by Jenna's own children.

The steady stream of visitors to the Wayfarer's Inn declined in the 1870s as the gold dwindled out, and Yale became the quiet place it had once been. Jenna and Matt, ever on the lookout for a new opportunity, sold the inn and purchased 100 acres on the Thompson River, in the heart of B.C.'s cattle country. Coming from an estate in England where horses were a part of life, Matt shared Jenna's dream of raising them. It wasn't long before they were meeting the demands of neighbouring cattle ranchers.

Their business thrived over the years. By the mid-1880s their ranch had expanded to 500 acres and they were not only raising horses, but running a guest house.

Matthew died in a canoeing accident at the age of seventy-four, leaving Jenna a widow at sixty. She was still spry and healthy and, once her year of mourning was over, she carried on the way Matt would have wanted her to. With her sons to take care of the horse-raising business and her daughter to help run the guest house, her time was spent going for long rides, exploring the countryside with her grandchildren, or visiting friends among her fellow ranchers.

Sitting bareback on a horse, the sun on her face,

and a river close by, it was easy to imagine herself riding on the prairie with Suzanne — in a way they had never been allowed to do — hoping to catch sight of a returning brigade.

A week before her seventy-fifth birthday, as she was about to go riding with her grandchildren, Jenna heard herself say that it was the last time they'd get her on a horse. They laughed, having heard it many times before. But on that July morning it turned out to be true.

Did Jenna ever write her Adventure Novel? No. But she filled numerous journals, and used her notes as the fuel for dozens of stories and articles. The stories — published in four separate volumes — covered her childhood on the prairie, her young adult life in Victoria and Metchosin, her married life as a gold miner and innkeeper during the Gold Rush years, and later, as a pioneer horse rancher in the interior of British Columbia.

The first collection of stories, published in 1880, was based on her early years growing up under the flag of the Hudson's Bay Company. Inspired by the Company's Latin motto *Pro Pelle Cutem* (roughly: a skin for a skin), she called the book *Pro Pelle Cutem: Tales from Inside the Stockade*. The first story, a favourite in her family, chronicled her time at Staines School in Fort Victoria. It was titled "Please, Sir — a Little Less Latin."

Historical Note

A tree-gnawing rodent, a fashion craze in Europe, and two fur traders from New France — who could have known that the merging of these elements would lead to the founding of an empire? Or that this empire would one day rule over half a continent and shape the western development of Canada? Small wonder that Canada's national animal is a beaver.

How did it come about?

In the early seventeenth century, the European fashion industry was booming. A huge demand for furs to trim clothing and to make hats made a waterproof beaver hat a must-have item, especially for well-heeled gentlemen.

The beaver's undercoat was so highly prized that early fur traders paid their best prices for furs that had been used until the long outer hairs had worn off, leaving the short barbed underhairs, which hatters shaved off the pelt and pressed into felt. This must have amused First Nations traders, who could exchange their old worn-out cloaks and get new European goods in return.

At first the fur trade was based in the growing settlement at Montreal. Independent traders, who came to be known as *voyageurs*, adopted the First Nations way of canoe travel and, with Huron partners acting as middlemen, took European goods to inland tribes, exchanged the goods for furs, and sold the furs to Montreal merchants for shipment to France. The system worked well until the Iroquois invaded Huron lands and the hostile environment made travelling those lands less safe.

Among the experienced *voyageurs* who traded with the First Nations were Pierre-Esprit Radisson and Médard Chouart des Groseilliers. Their inland journeys had convinced them that the greatest number of furs was to be found in the northern forests. In 1659 they travelled north of Lake Superior — farther than any *voyageurs* before them — and spent the winter with the Cree and Ojibwa. They learned the language, and discovered that, come spring, their hosts wanted to take their furs by a different route to avoid the fighting between the Huron and the Iroquois.

It made sense to the Frenchmen. Why travel through dangerous territory to ship furs by way of the St. Lawrence River, when the newly discovered Hudson Bay would serve as well, if not better? Such a route would make for easier travelling and enable the *voyageurs* to trade directly with their Cree and Ojibwa allies.

The authorities in Montreal were not interested in the idea — in fact, they arrested and fined the two men on their return for having set forth without a license — and neither was the king of France.

Undaunted, Radisson and Groseilliers went to London to put the proposal to King Charles II. The king gave them his support and, with the additional backing of Prince Rupert and a group of investors, the *voyageurs* set off in two British ships on June 3, 1668.

The ship carrying Radisson, the *Eaglet,* was forced to turn back, but the *Nonsuch,* with Groseilliers on board, arrived safely in Hudson Bay a month after leaving England. The crew beached the *Nonsuch,* built a shelter and, by preserving their catches of game and fish, were able to survive the harsh winter.

In spring, the Cree came downriver with their canoes heaped with beaver pelts. Gifts were exchanged and an alliance was formed. In mid-June the *Nonsuch* returned to England laden with beaver pelts. The expedition's investors were so impressed they pooled their money to form a new company and, on May 2, 1670, King Charles II authorized a Royal Charter creating The Governor and Company of Adventurers of England Trading into Hudson's Bay. The Hudson's Bay Company was born.

The Royal Charter promised that the founders of the Company would be "true and absolute Lordes and Proprietors of Rupert's Land." In essence, they had ownership of all the land drained by all the rivers flowing into Hudson Bay — an amazing forty percent of modern Canada, stretching from what is now Quebec, to Alberta, north into today's North West

Territories and south into what is now the United States.

FUR WARS

The trading methods of the French *voyageurs* to the south and the English "Bay Men" in the north differed greatly. The Bay Men manned remote trading posts strategically placed at Hudson Bay. They did not go inland to collect the furs, but waited for brigades of Cree, Ojibwa, Chipewyan and others to bring the furs to them. Once a year, a Company ship would arrive from London, anchor at York Factory at the mouth of the Hayes River, unload its supplies and trade goods, and sail away with its cargo of furs. Given its location on the Hayes River — a virtual highway to the prime beaver country — York Factory (so named because it housed the Company's Chief Factor of the area) was the Company's most valuable post.

Unlike the Bay Men, the *voyageurs* of New France went out to get the furs. With the coming of the HBC, however, they began to push farther inland, seeking more trading partners. Sometimes they would waylay First Nations traders and bargain for their furs, to prevent the competing Bay Men from getting them. The rivalry between the two groups intensified after the end of the Seven Years War in 1763, with New France now in the hands of Great Britain.

British businessmen began to settle in Montreal, and young Scottish immigrants joined *voyageur* brigades. During the winter of 1783–84, Montreal merchants and traders banded together to fight the HBC by founding the North West Company, whose traders were commonly known as the Nor'Westers. In response, Bay Men broke with their hundred-year-old tradition and moved from the Bay into the beaver country.

As competition between the trading companies further intensified, the well-being of First Nations people began to suffer. The arrival of the HBC with its trade goods had at first benefitted First Nations — items such as steel tools and traps and copper cooking pots had a huge impact on both men and women in making their daily lives easier — but as a trading hook in its fight against the North West Company, the HBC had turned to alcohol. The effects on a people who had no history with alcohol were devastating.

Adding to the disastrous effects of alcohol addiction were the white men's diseases. First Nations had no immunity to diseases such as smallpox, and the epidemics that swept the country at various times claimed a staggering toll on the local populations. In the smallpox epidemic of 1837, for instance, some three-quarters of the Plains people perished.

Competition forced the fur trade both farther west and farther north, with each side building new trading posts and making new alliances with First Nations groups. Following the expeditions of Nor'Westers such as Peter Pond, Alexander Mackenzie, David Thompson and Simon Fraser, the North West Company established posts as far west as the Pacific Coast.

Eventually, both companies began losing money, from supporting too many forts and buying too many pelts — mostly to keep the other side from getting them. The rivalry came to a head in 1816 when the governor of Lord Selkirk's colony at Red River, as well as twenty settlers, were shot down by allies of the Nor'Westers during the Battle at Seven Oaks.

Five years later the fur-trade war came to an end. Although the Nor'Westers had gone farther and fought harder, they were ultimately no match for the wealthier Hudson's Bay Company with its friends in the British government. An act of British Parliament merged the two companies in 1821, under the name The Hudson's Bay Company, with George Simpson as Governor. In a few years, Montreal's two-hundred-year-old fur trade died away. The HBC now had a trading empire that stretched from Labrador to the Pacific Coast — more than half the area of present-day Canada.

NEW FORTS ON THE PACIFIC

Although competition with the North West Company had ended with the merger, the HBC was not without its rivals. In its Columbia District (also known as the Oregon Territory), the United States was challenging British trade. American settlers were flooding into the area and, although the Oregon Territory was jointly occupied by the U.S. and Britain, there was growing concern among the British that the Americans would drive the HBC away from the Columbia River, and that once the U.S. boundary was established, British forts would end up on the American side. Fort Vancouver, established in 1825 as the HBC's base on the Pacific, would therefore have to be replaced.

With this in mind, Simpson sent Fort Vancouver's Chief Factor, James Douglas, to find a suitable site on the southern end of Vancouver Island, a region Simpson had previously visited and considered promising. Within a year Douglas had found the site, located in an area he described in a letter as "a perfect Eden."

On the night of March 15, 1843 (and for several nights following), a spectacular comet streaked across the sky over the southern tip of Vancouver Island. Among those who witnessed the astonishing cosmic event were the Songhees (Lekwungen), a group of Coast Salish First Nations. The event may have been especially memorable for them, given that a day earlier, a small steamship named the *Beaver* had dropped its anchor in a sheltered harbour in Songhees territory and fired its cannon. The Songhees welcomed the *Beaver* and her passengers, cutting stakes and providing logs for the new fort, and supplying firewood and food such as berries and salmon. By the end of 1843, Fort Victoria, (now Victoria, B.C., named after the young queen) was established.

Three years later, Britain yielded the Oregon Territory, including Fort Vancouver (now Vancouver, Washington), to the United States. Fort Victoria consequently became the Company's new Pacific headquarters. In 1849 Richard Blanshard was appointed Governor of the newly established Colony of Vancouver Island and, in June of that year, James Douglas was posted to Fort Victoria as its Chief Factor.

LIFE WITH THE HUDSON'S BAY COMPANY

A Regulated Workforce

From the beginning, the Company was run along the lines of a military establishment, though few of its employees were trained in the use of arms. They were basically divided into two classes — officers and servants — and their life was one in which everyone knew his place. The Chief Factor was the senior officer at each fort, followed by Chief Trader and Clerk. (In the case of smaller posts, the Chief Trader would assume the duties of Factor.) The Chief Factor was responsible for his post, and for trading with the First Nations, although the actual bartering for pelts was done by his Chief Trader, often assisted by a Clerk and Clerk's apprentice.

Unlike the officers, who were expected to have a

career with the Company, servants were engaged under contract, for periods of five years (hence the term *engagé* when referring to the French-Canadian servants). They were then paid off and were free to return on the annual ship or sign on for an additional period. Wages for employees, whether officers or servants, were not high, but the employees did receive free board and lodging. Besides, given the remoteness of most forts, there was little to spend money on.

The labourers, the lowest of the servant class, were employed to do the tough physical work — hauling lumber, cutting firewood, unloading supplies and trade goods from the annual ship and reloading it with pelts. The best-paid and highest-ranking servants were the skilled craftsmen and tradesmen — carpenters, joiners, boat builders, blacksmiths, tinsmiths, coopers, stewards, cooks, bakers, storekeepers — the backbone of the workforce, who produced a wide range of trade goods and supplies for the post.

Daily life at a fort was regulated by the use of a bell to signal changes in work routine — a practice borrowed from the Royal Navy, and considered to be a symbol of a disciplined and punctual workforce.

Pro Pelle Cutem

Everything revolved around the fur trade. In spring, First Nations traders would arrive, their canoes filled with furs, to be greeted with great ceremony by the

Chief Factor or, in smaller posts, the Chief Trader. Gifts would be exchanged. Only then would the trading begin.

The process could take many days. Each man's pelts were carefully examined by the Chief Trader. He noted their quality and paid the individual not in cash, but with "Made Beaver," the currency of the fur trade and the standard by which everything else was measured. All skins were compared to a prime-quality beaver pelt properly stretched and tanned and weighing about a pound (half a kilogram), and valued accordingly.

Made Beaver (MB) were usually given as wooden — or later, copper — tokens, and could be exchanged for items in the Company's trade store. Two otter skins might be valued as 1 MB, but for martens, three skins would be required for 1 MB. After receiving his MB in exchange for the pelts, an individual could exchange them for goods at the trade store. He might need 9 MB for 3 yards (about 3 metres) of cloth, and 11 MB for a gun. Other popular items were kettles, beads, tobacco, tools and wool blankets — one of which could require 7 MB.

After trading, the pelts were taken to the fur loft above the Trade Room and assembled into "pieces" — each "piece" being a bale of pelts packed within a frame and bound with cord, with a weight of about 90 pounds (40 kilograms). Once the rivers were clear of ice, brigades would set out from their forts to York Factory on Hudson Bay. Their arrival would coincide with that of the home ship, a ship that sailed from London each summer to deliver supplies and pick up the pelts.

Although the HBC acquired posts on the Pacific after the merger, the overland route to Hudson Bay continued to be used. The supply routes were already in place and the cost of using ships to transport furs and supplies by way of Cape Horn (at the tip of South America) was deemed too expensive. As for the time involved, the return journey from the HBC's base on the Pacific Coast, around Cape Horn, then northeast across the Atlantic to London, could take over a year.

Many officers, however, were in favour of having the posts west of the Rockies serviced by ships. After years of discussion and various attempts to find a suitable brigade route to the coast, it was eventually decided that it was worth a try. By the late 1840s brigades from the New Caledonia District (present-day British Columbia) and the Columbia District (now northern Washington State) were travelling by pack horse and boat to Fort Vancouver on the Columbia River and later, after the U.S. border was established, to Fort Langley on the Fraser, where coastal steamers would unload the European goods and supplies for the inland posts, and transport the District's exports (furs, salmon and cranberries) to the home ship anchored at Fort Victoria.

The route through the Rocky Mountains continued to be used as circumstances required — by
employees moving to a new post, for instance, or by
small parties transporting leather goods, or carrying
communications such as letters or post accounts.

Given the loads they were carrying, the men of
the brigades had to travel light. They hunted for
fresh game whenever possible, but depended on
pemmican for food, stopping to replenish their supply at strategically-located pemmican caches. Pemmican was perfect for long journeys. It never seemed
to go bad, and it could be eaten as was, made into a
soup, or covered with flour and fried. It was healthy,
too — especially with the addition of dried saskatoon
berries to fight off scurvy.

Both horse and boat brigades travelled on a regular schedule (or as regular a schedule as possible,
depending on the weather) and, to the residents of
the Company's remote posts, they meant more than
the outward transport of pelts and the inward flow
of provisions, for they were a vital link to the outside world. Letters to family and friends went out
with the brigades and replies came back the same
way — six months or so later. For letters to and
from London, the waiting could take over a year
and a half. Mail on the Pacific Coast was carried
throughout the year by coastal ships like the *Beaver*,
and sometimes by canoes manned by First Nations
paddlers.

Partners in the Fur Trade

For almost two hundred years the fur trade played a major role in shaping the history of Western Canada, not only economically but socially. Through a blending of First Nations and European traditions, a distinctive society developed with a set of customs unique to the fur trade. A prime example was *mariage à la façon du pays* (marriage in the custom of the country).

The custom began with the early French traders, continued with the men of the North West Company and, later on, the men of the Hudson's Bay Company. The HBC at first forbade their officers or servants to form relationships with First Nations women, but eventually they too realized what their competitors had known long ago: the success of the fur trade depended on a partnership with the First Nations, for each group had something the other wanted — furs, interpreters and guides on one side, European goods on the other. And that trading partnership could be strengthened through marriage.

Such unions benefitted both groups. Traders were drawn into the kinship circles of their First Nations wives and could therefore build more favourable trading relationships. First Nations relatives could gain better access to the posts and trade goods. The women themselves could take advantage of the goods that made their working lives easier.

After marriage, First Nations women continued to perform their traditional roles, their skills being crucial to the running of the fort. They made moccasins, the most practical footwear for the wilderness, and snowshoes, which made winter travel possible. They were skilled in handling canoes and helped to make them, by collecting the spruce roots and spruce gum needed for sewing the seams and for caulking. In winter, they augmented the food supply at the posts by snaring small game such as rabbits and squirrels. They played an important role in preserving food, especially in the making of pemmican, the staple of the canoe brigades and, in posts throughout the Plains, they worked to ensure that the annual quota of pemmican was met. They also made the buffalo-hide sacks needed to store and transport the pemmican, ensuring that each sack was filled with the required 90 pounds.

Mariage à la façon du pays had more than economic advantages. Since there were no white women in Western Canada for over a hundred years after white men arrived, and since most traders spent much of their lives in the wilderness, the only way they could have a family life was to take a First Nations wife.

Until the union of the two fur trading companies in 1821, *mariage à la façon du pays* was an informal arrangement, more in keeping with First Nations traditions than European. The ritual involved the woman's consent, the consent of her relatives, and the payment of a bride price — often a horse, sometimes several hundred dollars worth of trade goods.

Once that had been settled, the couple would be escorted to the fort and recognized as man and wife, their marriage deemed to be as binding as any performed in a church.

By the early nineteenth century the fur trade society had begun to change. Marriage between Europeans and full-blood First Nations became less common as mixed-blood daughters came of age. These daughters had the best of both worlds — knowledge of traditional ways as taught by their mothers, and familiarity with European ways, as taught by their fathers. These young women, having grown up in a fur trade post, were ideally suited to serve as links between the two cultures and as interpreters for, in many cases, they were fluent in several First Nations languages.

It wasn't long before marriage between traders and mixed-blood women became the norm. The traditional *mariage à la façon du pays* gave way to a more European ritual, with the couple exchanging vows at a post before a Chief Factor or senior officer. After the union of the two companies, it became even more official, a form of civil marriage, in which the couple signed a marriage contract and agreed to be married by a clergyman at the first available opportunity. The contract, introduced by the HBC, also stressed the husband's economic responsibility.

Mariage à la façon du pays was widespread among officers. In 1828, for example, James Douglas, then stationed at Fort St. James, took sixteen-year-old Amelia Connolly, the daughter of a Chief Factor and a Cree woman, as a country wife, and made her his legal wife thirteen years later. Amelia bore him thirteen children and lived to become Lady Douglas when her husband was knighted in 1863.

The often lonely and monotonous life of a fur trader, and the severe winters he had to endure, were undoubtedly made bearable by having a wife and children — or what Douglas, a devoted family man, called "the many tender ties."

Fur trade fathers took an active role in their children's upbringing, especially during the long winter months when they were more often at the fort, and were encouraged to give them a basic education that included Christian virtues. They were particularly mindful of their daughters for, unlike the boys, the girls were seldom sent overseas to further their education. Instead, they were groomed for a good marriage, preferably with an incoming trader of the officer class. Many such traders undoubtedly furthered their career prospects by marrying a senior officer's daughter.

The most significant changes in fur trade society began with the arrival of missionaries and white women. Missionaries considered *mariage à la façon du pays* to be immoral, and judged native women according to European standards. And with the marriage of Governor Simpson to a young English lady in 1830, traders began to look at white wives as status symbols, despite the fact that such women were extremely ill-prepared to handle a wilderness life.

By the mid-1800s, the "custom of the country" had become a custom of the past and was no longer acceptable. In more settled areas, such as the Red River Colony, native skills were no longer required. European women considered themselves superior to mixed-blood women, and the already-entrenched class system of the HBC became all the more apparent.

As for the First Nations wives, what became of them when their husbands left Rupert's Land, as many eventually did? Though some traders abandoned their native families with no second thoughts, others did so reluctantly, recognizing that their wives would find it difficult to adapt to a life in the Canadas or overseas. What's more, wives who had spent their lives inside a trading post might find it difficult to return to life with their tribe. The social problem that resulted gave rise to a custom known as "turning off," whereby a retiring husband might seek to have his wife marry, or his family come under the protection of, another trader.

Many traders remained loyal to their native families and, judging by the private correspondence that has survived, expressed affection towards their wives and children. Concerned about their future, they put money in trust to support their families in case of death or after they left the Company. They endeavoured to find employment for their sons within the Company, and suitable husbands for their daughters — preferably among Company employees.

THE END OF AN ERA

In 1858 gold was discovered in the Fraser River and, when the first gold reached San Francisco in early April, the Fraser River Gold Rush was on. For miners coming from the United States, Victoria was the first stop. Almost overnight, gold prospecting became the major industry in that part of the HBC's territory and, to formalize its hold on the Pacific Coast, Britain established the Colony of British Columbia. James Douglas, after severing his ties with the HBC, was appointed Governor in November 1858, thus becoming the Governor of Vancouver Island and British Columbia.

In 1869, two years after the Confederation of Canada and almost two hundred years after the HBC had received its Charter, the Company sat down with the British and Canadian governments to barter away its monopoly of trade and its vast territorial holdings in North America. Just over a century later, in 1970 — in celebration of its three-hundredth anniversary — the HBC headquarters was moved from London to Canada — a fitting move for a Company that had long been a Canadian icon.

A number of people who appear in Jenna's diary were historical figures. Their names are listed below. Another historical figure mentioned in the diary is George Simpson, Governor of the HBC.

At Fort Edmonton:
John Rowand, Rev. Robert T. Rundle, Paul Kane

At Jasper House:
Colin Frazer

At Fort Colvile and Fort Langley:
Alexander Caulfield Anderson, James and Eliza Anderson, James Murray Yale, Aurelia and Bella Yale

At Fort Victoria:
James Douglas, Amelia Douglas, Rev. Robert Staines, Mrs. Emma Staines, Horace Tahourdin, Roderick Finlayson, Dr. Alfred Benson, James Yates and Mrs. James Yates, Dr. John Sebastian Helmcken, Governor Richard Blanshard, Frédèrique Minie, Jacques Beauchamp, Rev. Honoré-Thimothée Lempfrit, Mr. Field

At Staines School:
Four Douglas sisters, including Jane Douglas (who is mentioned by name), four girls and a boy from the Work family, James and Eliza Anderson

Epilogue:
Captain Langford and his family, Martha Cheney

[ne] first page of the Charter that formed the Hudson's Bay Company in
[M]ay 1670, granting it exclusive trading rights to all the land in the
[H]udson Bay watershed — an enormous area comprising over a third of
[pr]esent-day Canada.

Made-Beaver (MB)
tokens. Through a
die-maker's error, *N*
instead of *M* appears
at the bottom of the
token "face" shown
on the right. The
tokens were about
the size of a twonie.

Paul Kane painted Fort Edmonton during his visit there in 1846. The large house rising above the stockade is the residence of Chief Factor John Rowand. In the foreground stands a Home Guard Cree encampment. The horse is dragging a *travois*, a frame used by Plains tribes for carrying loads.

Transporting furs and supplies to and from York Factory would have been impossible without light but sturdy canoes, and the skill of the paddlers who manned them.

Voyageurs paddled many hours a day, stopping at times for *une pipée* — the amount of time it would take to smoke a pipe.

Voyageurs made annual expeditions to take furs to Hudson
Bay — a huge distance that often involved hauling cargo and
canoes around unnavigable rivers. Portages were feats of
endurance that required great stamina.

Heavy York boats, so-called because they were first built at York Factory, could carry three times as much cargo as a large canoe. Unlike canoes, however, they could not be carried on a portage but had to be dragged over log rollers. Fort Edmonton eventually became the centre for York boat construction, and boat builders from the Orkney Islands were hired for that purpose.

The HBC Trade Store was where First Nations people would come to trade. Here they exchanged Made-Beaver tokens (received in exchange for pelts) for European goods.

Furs and pelts were stored in a post's fur loft, where they would be weighed, pressed and packed into bales called "pieces," in preparation for transport. Animals were usually trapped in winter, when their fur was at its thickest.

Encampment, Foot of the Rocky Mountains

Brigades that had crossed the Rockies on horseback and by foot via the Athabasca Pass would eventually reach Boat Encampment on the Columbia River. From there, they would continue their journey to the Pacific in boats specifically brought up for that purpose from Fort Vancouver.

A Songhees village located across the harbour from Fort Victoria. (Below) A Songhees woman weaving. Special white "wool" dogs (now extinct) were shorn and their hair mixed with mountain-goat wool to create the blankets.

The family of Alexander Caulfield Anderson. James and Eliza feature in Jenna Sinclair's fictional diary. James's unpublished recollections included stories of his days at Staines School.

This sketch of the interior of Fort Victoria shows the southeast corner of the yard. Bachelors' Hall, with Staines School and the dormitories, is the second building from the left.

VANCOUVER ISLAND.—THE HUDSON BAY COMPANY'S ESTABLISHMENT.

Fort Victoria with the West Gate facing the harbour and the Songhees village on the left. The 8-sided bastion is on the right, as well as sections of the Company's farm. In a letter dated June 21, 1844, Sir George Simpson stated that the country and the climate were "remarkably fine" and that the place "would become important."

275

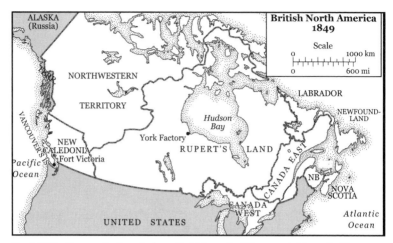

In 1849, Rupert's Land dwarfed Canada West and Canada East. The boundary with the United States had just been drawn in 1846.

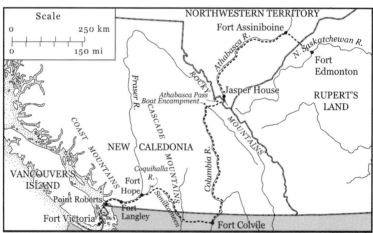

Small brigades sometimes travelled from Fort Edmonton to the Pacific via the Columbia River. After 1846, brigades in New Caledonia began to use a new route, following the Fraser River from Fort Hope to Fort Langley. From there, pelts were shipped to Fort Victoria.

276

Acknowledgments

Grateful acknowledgment is made for permission to reprint the following:

Cover portrait: Detail from *The Little Knitter 1884* by William Bouguereau.
Cover background: Detail from *View of Victoria, Vancouver Island.* Drawn by H. O. Tiedemann. T. Picken, lith. Created/published London, Day & Son, 1860, U.S. Historical Archive.

Page 263 (upper): *The Hudson's Bay Company Charter.* The Hudson's Bay Company Charter is a trade-mark of, and reproduced with the permission of, Hudson's Bay Company. Image courtesy of Hudson's Bay Company, Archives of Manitoba HBCA 1987/363-C-25/6.

Page 263 (lower): *HBC made-beaver tokens from Eastmain,* Hudson's Bay Company Archives/Archives of Manitoba HBCA 1987/363-M-39/5.

Page 264: *Fort Edmonton,* Paul Kane. With permission of the Royal Ontario Museum © ROM.

Page 265: *Running a Rapid on the Mattawa River,* C. Butterworth, engraver, after Frances Anne Hopkins, Library and Archives Canada, C-013585.

Page 266: Detail from *Voyageurs at Dawn,* Frances Anne Hopkins, Library and Archives Canada Acc. No. 1989-401-3, C-134839.

Page 267: *At the Portage, Hudson's Bay Company's Employees on their annual Expedition,* H.A. Ogden, Library and Archives Canada C-082974.

Page 268: *York boat under sail near Norway House, Manitoba, 1913;* photographer: R.A. Talbot, Hudson's Bay Company, Archives of Manitoba HBCA 1987/363-Y-2/56 (N14645).

Page 269: *Indians Trading Furs, 1785,* C.W. Jefferys, Library and Archives Canada C-73431.

Page 270: *The Fur Loft at a Hudson's Bay Post,* Beckles Willson, Taken from *The Great Company,* pub. 1900, Hudson's Bay Company Archives, 1987/363-F-225/2 (N81-221E).

Page 271: *Boat Encampment, 1846* (sketch), Paul Kane, Stark Museum of Art, Orange, Texas WWC 100; CR IV-276.

Page 272 (upper): *A Sangeys Village on the Esquimalt, 1847* (sketch), Paul Kane, Stark Museum of Art, Orange, Texas WWC 66; CR IV-526.

Page 272 (lower): *Interior of a Lodge with Indian Woman Weaving a Blanket, 1847* (sketch), Paul Kane, Stark Museum of Art, Orange, Texas WWC 73; CR IV-552.

Page 273: *Alex Caulfield Anderson's sons* [sic] *and daughters,* B.C. Archives Collections, A-07789, Acc. No. 193501-001.

Page 274: *Interior of the Hudson's Bay Company fort No. 2,* Sarah Crease, B.C. Archives Collections PDP02892, Acc. No. 199104-002.

Page 275: *Vancouver Island — the Hudson's Bay Company's Establishment, 1848 (Fort Victoria),* Hudson's Bay Company, Archives of Manitoba P-164 (N5350).

Page 276: Maps by Paul Heersink/Paperglyphs. Map data © 2002 Government of Canada with permission from Natural Resources Canada.

We thank the Hudson's Bay company for its co-operation and contribution in allowing us permission to use the company trade-mark on page 263.

Thanks to Dr. Sylvia Van Kirk, author of *Many Tender Ties,* for her expert advice and guidance, particularly regarding the importance of First Nations women during the fur trade era. We are grateful to her book and her many articles, which form the basis of "Partners in the Fur Trade" in the Historical Note.

Thanks to Barbara Hehner for her careful checking of the manuscript; to Tyrone Tootoosis for his assistance with the Cree sections; and to Sylvia Olsen for her advice re the Songhees sections. Thanks also to Michael Payne, City Archivist of Edmonton, and James Gorton of the HBC Archives, as well as to Dr. Bill Waiser and his colleagues (Dr. Carolyn Podruchny, Dr. Nicole St-Onge, Jim McKillip and Robert Englebert) for weighing in on what we thought would be a straightforward question: What route did the brigades usually travel?

Three sources were particularly helpful during the writing of this book: the unpublished recollections of James Anderson, former student of Staines School, *The Reminiscences of Doctor John Sebastian Helmcken,* and *Fort Victoria Letters, 1846–1851,* written by James Douglas and published by the Hudson's Bay Records Society.

Nancy J. Turner, Professor, and Dr. Brenda Beckwith, School of Environmental Studies, University of Victoria, were invaluable sources of information concerning camas, as was Cheryl Bryce, Lands Manager of the Songhees First Nation.

I am grateful to Dr. Sylvia Van Kirk for her generosity in lending me books, recommending reading material and providing me with copies of her articles. Through her writings, I came to appreciate the significant role played by First Nations women in fur trade society, and how the very existence of that society may have been a reason why the history of Western Canada was so different from that of the "Wild West" of the United States.

Once again I had the good fortune to work with my gifted editor, Sandy Bogart Johnston. Her unwavering support, patience and humour made her a "Chief Factor" par excellence throughout the writing of this book.

To Patrick, who held the fort
during my HBC sojourn
and sustained me with an abundance of treats
and laughter

About the Author

Much of *Where the River Takes Me* is set in Julie Lawson's very own neighbourhood. She lives in the area that was once the HBC's Fort Victoria and its surroundings, near Beacon Hill and the camas meadows and what was once Beckley Farm — places explored by her character Jenna. Nothing remains of Fort Victoria itself, but "I can walk around the perimeter of where the stockade once stood (the east side, on Government Street, is marked by bricks in the sidewalk), and see the exact spots where the belfry stood, Bachelors' Hall with the dormitories and Staines School, the west gate leading to the water and the east gate opening onto Fort Street (once a dirt road leading out to the HBC farms). I can look at the Empress Hotel, make it disappear in my mind and see the mud flats of James Bay. I can walk around the Bay, cross the stream, and continue on to Beacon Hill."

The research for this book, because it involved several HBC forts, was a huge challenge, involving a number of different historical advisors. Julie got so deeply into the research that she found herself "unintentionally talking like Jenna and writing emails using her voice. I went blank when I picked up the phone, not knowing where I was. I wrote 1850 on cheques. I dream-walked to town and along Victoria's waterfront, my body here, but my mind on a brigade route somewhere else."

Julie loves the spring, when the camas in Beacon Hill Park is in bloom. She says that "the meadows that remain literally shimmer with blue. . . . My research into that aspect of Songhees life was fascinating and involved talking to local experts — two ethnobotanists and the land manager of the Songhees (Lekwungen) First Nation. The way the First Nations tended the camas — the harvesting, weeding, burning after the harvest, and the cooking — gave me a new appreciation for that part of their culture." She also learned "that a side effect of eating camas is flatulence. And if you eat the bulb of white camas (which looks the same as blue camas) the side effect is death."

The research was truly daunting. "I used to tell school groups that I loved doing research. That was before the HBC (Horrendously Big Challenge). The problem with researching the HBC was that I liked it too much. It was all so interesting! And overwhelming. The number of books, articles, websites, etc. related to the HBC, the North West Company, the fur trade in general, the journals kept by the different explorers — there is an endless source of material. I get excited just thinking about it."

Julie's overall interest in the HBC was further boosted when she came across the unpublished recollections of James Anderson, while researching a different book. "James was only nine years old when he travelled from Fort Colvile to Fort Langley with a fur brigade, accompanied by his father and his sister. He and his sister Eliza, age twelve, actually crossed the rough Strait of Georgia by canoe — just as they and Jenna do in this story — and they attended Staines School. The details that James remembers and describes are amazing. It goes without saying that they were an inspiration. How I wish Eliza had written her memoirs of that period!"

For years Julie has been the proud owner of an HBC coat that she bought at a church thrift shop when she was writer-in-residence in Dawson City, Yukon. "It cost an unbelievable 15 Made Beaver." She also has a *ceinture fléchée*, which she plans to wear on school visits when talking about *Where the River Takes Me*.

Julie is the author of two prior Dear Canada books, *No Safe Harbour* (winner of the 2008 Hackmatack Award) and *A Ribbon of Shining Steel* (finalist for the CLA Book of the Year Award). Since she left teaching to become a full-time writer, she has published over twenty-five books, including *The Pirates of Captain McKee* (finalist for the Governor General's Award for illustration), *The Dragon's Pearl* (finalist for the Ruth Schwartz and CLA Book of the Year Awards), and *White Jade Tiger* (Sheila Egoff Award and CLA Honour Book). Other titles are *The Klondike Cat, Cougar Cove* and *The Ghost of Avalanche Mountain*.

National Library of Canada Cataloguing in Publication

Lawson, Julie, 1947—
Where the river takes me : the Hudson's Bay Company diary of
Jenna Sinclair, Fort Victoria, Vancouver's Island, 1850 / Julie Lawson.

(Dear Canada)
ISBN 978-0-439-95620-8

1. Hudson's Bay Company--Juvenile fiction. I. Title. II. Series.
PS8573.A94W48 2008   jC813'.54   C2008-900821-9

6 5 4 3 2 1   Printed in Canada   08 09 10 11 12

The display type was set in ITC Cheltenham Handtooled Bold Italic.
The text was set in Galliard.

First printing June 2008

Go to www.scholastic.ca/dearcanada for information on the Dear Canada Series — see inside the books, read an excerpt or a review, post a review, and more.